Short, Short Stories
and
Random Thoughts

Short, Short Stories and Random Thoughts

J. Willis Hurst, M.D.

To order additional copies of this book, contact:
Xlibris Corporation
1-888-795-4274
www.Xlibris.com
Orders@Xlibris.com
67677

CONTENTS

This book of short, short stories is dedicated with love to my wife, Nelie, who for sixty-two years brought happiness to our home

Preface

All lives are filled with stories, short stories, long stories, fun stories, sad stories, stories that teach, and stories that simply fill up space. The short, short stories reported here happened to Dr. Vance Connelly.

It's no longer a secret, Vance Connelly is the pen name of the author of this book, and Jennifer is the made-up name for his wife. I, the author, could not bring myself to use my real name in the stories. Those who have read, or have just seen, my previous books know that Dr. Vance Connelly is me. I know that, and they know that, but still, with two exceptions, I rebel at using my real name in all of the short, short stories contained in this little book. There would be too many Is for comfort.

Now, about this book. The stories are shorter than the usual short stories. Some are only a paragraph long, so the book is called *Short, Short Stories*. In fact, some of the stories are so short that I call them *random thoughts*. All of the stories actually happened during the eighty-nine years of my life. The conversations repeated in the stories may not be the exact words of those who spoke, and at times, the names of the people involved are changed, but the story lines always remain true. The stories are not arranged in any particular order because the author assumes the reader will delve into the book for an occasional quick read since each story, with its own unique message, stands alone.

The reader will notice that the style of writing differs according to the story. Sad writing goes with a sad story; and fun writing, one with catchy metaphors, goes with a fun story. Most of the stories were written recently, but some were written twenty and forty years ago. Writing styles, like people, change over the years. So the reader will notice that the style of writing is not consistent.

I wish to thank my daughter-in-law, Leslie Hurst, who typed the manuscript. She is good at everything she does and knows no strangers. Without her, there would be no book.

Finally, I miss my wife, Nelie (Jennifer), who was not only beautiful but also had a beautiful view of the world and made my life whole. I wrote in the preface of my previous books, no Nelie, no book. Since she is indelibly stamped in my memory, I write again, no Nelie, no book.

J. Willis Hurst, M.D.
St. Simons Island

1

The Young Valet, Walter Mitty,

and Haile Selassie

"I gotta Porsche." The valet shrugged his shoulders. His English was better than most Americans', and his voice was as smooth as Sinatra's. "In fact, I have two Porsches. I come to work in the old one and leave the new one at home." He waited to observe the reaction to his words. His timing was carefully planned and competed well with Jack Benny. "I am rich, you see— very, very rich. I don't need to work. I just do it for fun." He must have detected a doubtful look on Vance's face because he reached in his pocket and pulled out a huge roll of ten-dollar bills, enough to choke a cow, and muttered again, "I'm rich."

The young valet was talking to Dr. Vance Connelly who looked him over, up and down. Connelly, who walked with a cane, was simultaneously amused and perplexed. Never in his eighty-eight years had he heard such a story. He thought, *The young man is a valet who parks cars at the Brookland retirement community in Atlanta, Georgia. How could he be rich?*

Vance, of course, did not believe the Walter Mitty story, but played along with it because it dampened his sorrow that developed and persisted after his wife died. He squinted his eyes and studied the young valet who sported a Barack Obama haircut, an embryonic mustache on his upper lip, and a square inch of short black hair on his chin. All of this, plus his black jacket, made him fit for the movies.

The valet and his partners not only parked cars, but they sensed the needs of the people who lived at Brookland, Atlanta's premier retirement facility. They were kind, happy, and quick. They earned the praise of all of their charges.

The Porsche's owner introduced himself to Vance when he began working at Brookland. He said, "I am the great, great, grandson of Haile Selassie, the famous leader of Ethiopia." Vance doubted the claim, but from that day on, he called the valet Haile Selassie whenever he encountered him. Now, this young Haile Selassie was telling Vance he and all members of his family were very, very rich.

DJ, another very competent young valet from Ethiopia, with a short, narrow beard that traveled from his right ear, around his chin, to his left ear, joined Vance and Haile Selassie and volunteered that he had served two years in the army of Ethiopia. "Do you want to see the salute?" he asked with a large and happy grin.

Vance, who was enjoying the friendly competition for attention between the two valets, said, "Yes, yes, go ahead." With that, DJ stomped his right foot, then stomped his left foot, then stomped his right foot again. He then raised his right arm until his fingers touched his right eyebrow. This action was followed by a quick jerk of his head upward and backward. DJ beamed with pleasure and said, "Dr. Connelly, try it."

Vance tried but could not stomp his feet like DJ did. His action made no stomping noise. DJ made a sad expression, like a circus clown, and shook his head.

Samson, another excellent young Ethiopian valet, pulled Vance's car up so that Vance could make his daily trip to Greystone University Hospital where, at the age of eighty-eight, he continued to teach medical students, house officers, and cardiology fellows. He had done that for fifty-eight years, thirty as professor and chairman of the department of medicine.

Vance left his car at the emergency room entrance of Greystone University Hospital where another group of Ethiopian valets helped him. One, in particular, knew exactly how to walk beside Vance so Vance could place his left hand on the valet's right shoulder in order to steady his walking.

When Vance returned later in the day to Brookland, three Ethiopian valets saluted him simultaneously, and Vance struggled to return the salute. A few Brookland residents witnessed the act and appeared bewildered, like they had seen an unidentified flying object.

The next day, Vance thought he would expose Haile Selassie's made-up story, so he asked, "Did you come to work in one of your Porsches?"

Haile Selassie responded, "I came to work in my old Porsche."

Vance said, "I want to see your old Porsche. I will wait here for you."

Haile Selassie turned quickly and ran toward the parking area, which was out of Vance's sight. Vance waited and waited and waited. He asked Samson, "Is Haile Selassie coming back?"

Samson said, with his usual smile, "He probably can't locate a Porsche that belongs to one of the residents. If he could, he would bring it up here and claim it is his."

A few minutes later, Haile Selassie came panting up the little hill. Vance asked, "Where is the Porsche?"

"Oh Dr. Connelly," he hurriedly said as if he had no breath, "I thought you wanted to see it tomorrow. I am sorry, I did not understand, I am so sorry."

Vance said, appreciating Haile Selassie's award-winning act, "That's OK. I will see the Porsche another time."

The next day when Vance returned to Brookland from Greystone, Haile Selassie was waiting for him. Before Vance could ask about the Porsche, Haile Selassie said, "I am going to make you a new head for your walking stick. I will make it out of a solid gold bar."

Vance recognized another Walter Mitty story was on its way. Vance asked, "Is most of your enormous wealth in gold bars?"

"Yes, sir. That is why I must return to Ethiopia. We keep the gold bars in a vault in a bank, but we also have someone guard the vault twenty-four hours a day. We are so wealthy my family needs me to help them with the finances."

A few days later, Vance decided to ask Haile Selassie a simple question that would expose the young valet's fictive story. "So," Vance said, "Haile Selassie, I plan to write a little story about the excellent service you and your colleagues render here at Brookland. I am embarrassed to confess that I am not sure how to spell Haile Selassie. Would you help me?"

"Sure," he said as he pumped up his chest. "I will write it for you." With great assurance, he wrote *Haileselassie.*

Vance said in an alarmed voice, "You mean it's one word?" Vance thought he had finally exposed the true nature of his remarkable story.

"Yes sir, one word, not two."

Vance argued, "The *Encyclopedia Britannica* makes it two words."

"*Encyclopedia Britannica* is wrong," he answered with great confidence.

Later that day, Vance explained to two other Ethiopian valets that Haile Selassie had messed up. "He thought," said Vance with a hearty laugh, "that Haile Selassie was one word rather than two."

The two valets looked at each other, and then as if they regretted doing what they had to do, one of them said, "That's correct. In Ethiopia it's one word."

DJ, who had recently become a U.S. citizen, walked up, and Vance, who was beginning to believe his Walter Mitty friend, asked him, "Have you seen Haile Selassie's Porsches? If you say yes, I am planning to see a psychiatrist!"

DJ answered, "I saw his old Porsche—it was a 1991. It looked OK. But I have not seen his new one."

Vance threw up his arms and said, "You mean he really has one?" With that, Vance gave up. He was on his way to believing Haile Selassie.

DJ answered, "May not be his. He just said it was his."

With that, Vance again realized that the whole story was make-believe.

Dale and Matt, the two American valets, saw Vance and DJ talking. They wandered over. Dale was a first-rate businessman and did well in his job. Matt planned to finish college, but for now was having a great time, he could state the names of his girlfriends, one for each day of the week, as rapidly as a machine gun could shoot. In addition to Teddy, Dale, DJ, Samson, and Matt, there were Danny, Yonas, and Dave, all very competent and helpful in every way.

Vance asked, "Is Haile Selassie telling me the truth?"

Matt said as he squinted one eye, "He tells stories."

Vance waited and waited for his gold-headed cane and never got to see the Porsches, but he continued to make the salute. Vance thanked his Ethiopian friends, they were a constant cheer in the midst of all the problems our great country faces, and for a brief moment, they were able to trigger a rare, out-loud laugh by Vance who struggled mightily to cope with the loss of his wife.

2

That Tree Was Mine

Trees are the largest of nature's flowers. They come in all shapes, sizes, and colors. They really belong to no one—like the air, clouds, and water. Man tries to claim them, but they belong to Mother Nature. Having said that, Vance Connelly said to himself, "I agree, but there is one exception. *That* tree was mine."

Vance Connelly was looking at a splintered stump of a tree. It was located in the midst of a group of 150-year-old oaks. The massive disfigured old trees were located on the front campus of a university. One of the trees had been hit by lightning; only splinters were left.

Vance felt sad as he viewed the last remains of the beautiful flower, because he felt that *that* tree was his. He thought, *That particular tree was mine because that is where I first told my future wife that I loved her—we sat under that tree. She returned the sentiment. Surely, anyone can understand, that tree was mine. Now it is gone, as she is gone. But I can see her still sitting under that tree.*

3

Go Give Them a Speech

Vance Connelly, M.D. and Jennifer were sitting in the airport in Auckland, New Zealand. They had been in Australia for one week and New Zealand for three weeks as the guests of the combined heart associations of the two countries. Vance had given numerous talks at hospitals, medical meetings, organizations, television stations, and the equivalent of American grammar schools in many cities and numerous small towns. Despite the busy lecturing schedule about heart disease, Vance and Jennifer enjoyed the beautiful scenery and interesting people.

They were both reading, waiting for their plane, which would take them home to Atlanta. Jennifer, who had listened to all of Vance's speeches, was reading the newspaper as the area filled up with people. She looked over her reading glasses and said, "Vance, do you see that group of people over there? They look like they don't have anything to do. Why don't you go over there and give them a speech?"

4

The Visit

Sunday was a special day at Brookland. This act took place in the old Brookland, before the new wing was added to Atlanta's premier retirement facility. The scene occurred on Sunday at noon in the dining area where a buffet lunch was being served.

The two of them appeared at the dining room door. He held her hand and guided her to a table. Her makeup appeared to be crudely applied to her face. She did not smile, and her eyes seemed not to see. She sat motionless as he left her to fill both of their plates with food.

He was her gray-haired son, about sixty-five years old, twenty-five years younger than she, who had come to visit her. She was, she perfectly remembered at times, his mother.

He cut her food into small, bite-size pieces. She did not move, the vacant look continued. But she smiled a bit each time she turned her head and saw him, and placed her mouth toward the fork. Happiness was there for one brief moment.

She tired of his feeding her. He knew her signals. He helped her rise from table. She left with him, but noticed no one else, and undoubtedly wondered when her son, what was his name or was it a daughter, would come for a visit.

5

A Distinct Advantage*

Dr. Vance Connelly faced the junior medical school class in 1957 and announced that their final examination in medicine would be an open-book exam. He explained, "You can bring any books you wish to the exam and take as much time as you wish to answer the questions." The students gave a loud signal of approval. They applauded.

Dr. Vance Connelly had just begun his work as professor and chairman of the department of medicine at Greystone University Hospital. He was thirty-six years

---

* The core of this story is reproduced from J. W. Hurst, *Notes From a Chairman* (Chicago: Year Book Medical Publishers, Inc., 1987), 197-198. The author owns the copyright.

old and needed all the help he could muster to build a department of medicine. The students were distraught because so many faculty members had left the clinical departments. The students and house staff feared that their education was vanishing. They wondered what their new chief, Connelly, would do. They welcomed the idea of an open-book exam and apparently recognized the act as a good move by Vance.

Connelly knew the students would appreciate his effort to diminish their fear, but he had another reason for offering the students an open-book exam. He believed in self-learning. He recognized that no doctor could know everything. He also knew that a medical school faculty could not teach the students everything. He believed that the cornerstone of excellent medical education was to encourage individual students and young doctors to learn how to solve problems. A part of that effort should be the development of the skill for looking up the answers to self-generated questions in the appropriate books. So, his offer had a deeper meaning than the students realized.

Connelly felt good about the students' reception to his plan. He left the conference room with a smile and a quick step and returned to his office. In a few minutes, he heard a knock on his office door. He opened the door to discover one of the junior students he had just addressed. Connelly, a bit surprised, said, "Come in, have a seat on the sofa."

Connelly sat on the sofa, a comfortable distance from the student. He, being a doctor, observed that the student was pale (especially around his mouth) and seemed to be sweating profusely. The pupils of his eyes were dilated. He obviously was frightened. Connelly said, "What can I do for you?"

The student, with a trembling voice, said, "Dr. Connelly, that plan, an open-book examination, is the most unfair thing I have ever heard of."

Vance Connelly was shocked. His feelings sank in a second from feeling elated, to one of bewilderment. He said, "Please tell me what is unfair about giving an open-book examination."

Despite being as scared as a rabbit, the student was ready with an answer. He said, "Don't you see, the students who have been using the books all year will have a distinct advantage over the others."

Connelly, surprised beyond belief, pondered the indictment and finally addressed the student, "We will remember that point when we issue the grade."

6

Morning Report—Always—Anywhere

Morning report is a must in teaching hospitals. The medical trainees—medical students, interns, and residents who are planning to be internists or subspecialists in medicine, gather to review the problems of the patients who were admitted to the hospital during the previous twenty-four hours. The nascent physicians must be prepared to state the problems of the patients briefly, clearly, yet completely, to the senior physician in charge of the service.

Dr. Vance Connelly, in his role as professor and chairman of the department of medicine at Greystone University Hospital, was in charge of the morning report at Grady Memorial Hospital and Greystone University Hospital for many years.

This story is about a particular morning report that happened some forty years ago when trainees lived in the hospital and were on duty every third night.

The group of trainees, about twelve of them, met at 7:00 AM. Dr. Connelly expected every trainee to be present. He was never late and expected the trainees to always be on time.

One morning there were about fifteen admissions, and Vance wanted to hear the carefully selected details of the patients' problems. The trainee who had admitted three patients was not there to present his patients' problems.

Vance asked, "Where is Dr. Morgan? Is he ill?"

A colleague of Dr. Morgan's answered, "He is probably sleeping—he finished working with his last admission at 6:15 AM."

Vance had been waiting for an opportunity such as this. He said, "We will all go to his room in the house staff quarters and get him."

Dr. Morgan's associates thought that was a great idea. So Vance and the entire group of trainees went to Dr. Morgan's room. There he was, cuddled up in bed sound asleep. Vance and the group tiptoed to Dr. Morgan's backside. Vance very carefully pulled up a chair and sat next to the bed. Vance tapped Dr. Morgan on the shoulder until he opened his eyes, turned over, and saw Vance and his smiling colleagues. Dr. Morgan was a brilliant intern and, with it all, enjoyed himself immensely.

Vance said, "Sit on the side of the bed."

Dr. Morgan did so.

Vance said, "Let me help you put your little socks on."

Dr. Morgan did so.

Vance then said, "Let me help you put your little shoes on."

Dr. Morgan did so.

Vance said, "Now let us go down to morning report."

Dr. Morgan fumbled with his contact lenses and finally said, "Let's go."

They all returned to the conference room, and Vance said, "Dr. Morgan, present your patients to the group, and I would like for you to discuss the problems as well as present them. In other words, suppose you take over my role this morning."

Dr. Morgan did not bat an eye. He presented and discussed each one of his patients. His remarks were first rate. Vance, who had already been impressed by Dr. Morgan, was very pleased. Not only did he take the little joke in stride and enjoyed the event, but he was clearly the master of the moment.

Dr. Morgan finished his training. He was a brilliant, fun-loving guy. He rose to the top in the subspecialty of oncology.

7

Trust[*]

Graduation from medical school is a great event for students, parents, and faculty. Everyone congratulates the students on their accomplishments.

Vance points out to the students that when the diploma is placed in their hands, they have every right to be proud. They have worked hard. He also points out that they have received a gift from all of the physicians that have preceded them. Gift, they say. What gift? Vance answers that the *knowledge* they acquired during medical school was created by the physicians who came before them. More importantly, Vance points out the *trust* patients have in them was not created by

---

[*] Reprinted from J. Willis Hurst, *Essays From the Heart* (New York: Raven Press Publisher, 1995), 93-94. The author owns the copyright.

their own hard work. It was created by the physicians who preceded them. For centuries, physicians have proven to their patients that they could be *trusted*. The new graduate usually receives the gift of *trust* without considering how it came about.

Medical school graduates should realize that they must maintain the *trust* given to them when the diploma is placed in their hands. To this end, as the first step in establishing a *trust* relationship with patients, Vance emphasized the importance of the initial physician-patient encounter. The patient's history is, or should be, the starting point. There are two reasons why the patient's history is so important. The history reveals considerable medical information, but equally important, it is during the history-taking period that the physician must establish the bond of *trust* with the patient. The bond of *trust* is established by talking and listening. Such a bond is not established by machines. The new graduate earns individual *trustworthiness* using his or her talking and listening skills.

Should physicians establish a bond of *trust* during the initial encounter with their patients, they must be vigilant in their efforts to maintain it in the days, weeks, months, and years that follow. The relationship a physician has with the patient is unique, precious, and sacred and must never be violated. Physicians must demonstrate that they are concerned, honest, courteous, and that they are indeed the patient's advocate.

8

Reading

Everyone seems to agree that it is important for parents to read to their young children, even if the act helps the child to go to sleep. Vance also believed that it was equally important for the parents to eventually have the child read to them and for the child to express out loud the meaning of the sentences they read, because merely saying words is not reading.

Let us assume the child grows up and attends a famous university. There he or she may be exposed to lecture after lecture, often by a graduate student who may or may not be a true teacher, and hears him or her restate what is printed in a textbook. No wonder a high percentage of students go to sleep just as they did as a child. In addition, the "teacher" never knows if the students understand what he or she is saying, because a multiple choice exam does not determine if students can use the words they have heard in a thought process of their own.

Vance favored giving students an assignment in a book or a prepared document, having no lecture, and having each student, in private, answer this question, "Tell me in your own words what this paragraph means, and how does it fit in your knowledge base?"

Of course, if one thinks about it, this is why lectures are like your mother reading to you until you go to sleep. The brain is treated as a sponge, a poor sponge, rather than an active organ that functions best when it is asking questions and seeking solutions.

9

What Makes a Good Doctor

Good doctors place their patient's welfare first. They will inconvenience themselves rather than inconvenience their patients. They always consider the comfort of their patient and, above all, think about the safety of his or her patients. These attributes of good doctoring are not learned from books. They are instilled by the doctor's parents and role models. But copying won't do, the relationship being discussed here must be genuine and must be forever automatic.

Next, good doctors care enough about their patients to continue to study, as long as they see patients or teach young medical trainees. Self-study, the most important type of study, is self-generated by the doctors themselves. Their compassion leads to study. And study leads to competence. Good doctors may not know the answers to everything, but they know how to solve problems.

Note, it takes two very different things to be a good doctor—compassion for the patient and the constant struggle to improve his or her knowledge. One without the other spells failure.

10

Not Accepted[*]

Dr. Vance Connelly was sixty-five years old when he received the following letter.

Dear Dr. Connelly,

> We appreciate your desire to become a trainee in cardiology at our institution. We have numerous excellent applications to our popular cardiology program. We regret to inform you that you were not selected to join us.

---

[*] This story actually happened. The language used here is not exactly the same as that used twenty-three years ago, but the story is true.

The letter came from a great university, and the director of cardiology was known to be excellent. Vance recognized that a serious error had been made. He envisioned a busy secretary sitting behind stacks of paper. She made an error and somehow sent the letter to Vance when it should have been sent to the person who had applied to their cardiology training program. The director of cardiology at the famous institution, in haste, had signed the letter.

Vance was very pleased to have the letter. It gave him a chance to kid the director of cardiology—such happenings were rare, and Vance did not want to miss the opportunity. So he wrote the following letter:

Dear Dr.—,

I received your letter indicating that I had not been accepted to the cardiology training program at your great institution. I know you must have had numerous applications.

I had hoped that my background would make me reasonably competitive. I am currently 65 years old. I have my boards in cardiology. In fact, I was a member of the cardiology board for many years and was chairman of the board for three years. I have created several textbooks of cardiology—the best known is the book, *The Heart.* I am currently professor and chairman of the department of medicine at Greystone University and have had the opportunity and pleasure to train hundreds of cardiologists. I had hoped this background would qualify me for a training position at your institution.

I am disappointed that I was not selected, but will study more and work hard to convince you to accept me next year.

Sincerely,
Vance Connelly, M.D.

Vance received no subsequent letters from the institution. He envisioned the secretary quietly shredding his letter. Vance smiled, for the whole event brought silent laughter to him.

11

A Very Strange Event

Dr. Vance Connelly was home, sitting in his favorite chair, talking to his wife, Jennifer. The hour was about 10:00 PM.

The telephone rang its piercing, but familiar, and compelling call.

Vance picked up the phone. "Vance," the caller said, as if it were his last breath, "this is Jerry—remember me? We went to school together."

"Yes. Yes. What's up, Jerry? Good to hear from you."

Jerry responded, "I am seriously ill. I have just had cardiac arrest."

Vance asked, "What do you mean? You are talking to me, you can't be having cardiac arrest. Where are you?"

"I am lying on the floor pressing on the middle of my chest thirty times a minute."

"Jerry, you are not making sense." Vance was beginning to realize that Jerry's trouble was not his heart, but emotional-psychiatric. He asked, "Jerry, I think I had better check you out in person. Can you meet me at the emergency room at Greystone University Hospital?"

Jerry answered, "Sure, I'll be there in a few minutes. I am still resuscitating myself."

Vance hugged Jennifer and drove rapidly to the emergency room. He worried that his old friend would have to be admitted to the psychiatric floor of the hospital.

Vance arrived at the emergency room. He told Grace, an experienced emergency room nurse, the story.

She, with her wisdom, said, "Dr. Connelly, he won't come. You are wasting your time."

Grace was right. He did not come. Vance has not seen or heard from Jerry since this phone call. Vance always said it was one of the most unusual experiences he had during his long career.

12

Entertainment during the Great Depression

Vance Connelly grew up in a small town. When he was about ten years old, the depression of the 1930s was in full force. There was very little entertainment in the home, except books to read. Vance remembers reading Tom Swift, The Rover Boys, The Hardy Boys, Tom Sawyer, Huckleberry Finn, poems by Tennyson, Longfellow, and stories by Edgar Allan Poe. He also remembers quotations uttered by one particular teacher. Vance's father was principal of his school; and his aunt, who lived with them, was his teacher.

Vance's only entertainment outside the home was at the movie theater and the courthouse. His only source of fun money was cutting the grass. He made ten cents cutting the grass on Saturday mornings. He went to the movie theater in the afternoon. It cost ten cents if you were twelve or younger and twenty-five cents if you were over twelve. He met his friends there and sat on the front row and watched Tom Mix, Buck Jones, Hoot Gibson, Ken Manard, Tim McCoy ride horses, shoot guns, win the girls, and ride off into the sunset on beautiful white horses. At that age, all Vance and his friends wanted to do was to see cowboys. They did not venture into the theater during the week to see the famous stars of the era. Vance vividly recalls his sadness when he turned thirteen and was told he must pay twenty-five cents, instead of ten cents, to see the movie.

Vance's other entertainment was at the courthouse. The new courthouse was simply beautiful, and when court was in session, it was as busy as a beehive. Vance would go to the large courtroom, sit on the back row, listen to the local lawyers argue, observe the jury, wonder what they were going to do, and observe the families who sat near the front, and tried to determine what the verdict should be. He learned two important lessons: the difference in circumstantial evidence and direct evidence, and that the information given in both categories could be wrong. He marveled at the brilliance of the lawyers and how they could sway the jurors. Some of the lawyers would quote poetry and even cry a little to drive home their argument.

When Vance turned fifteen, he went to the movie during the week and would go to the Green Front. This was the only fast-food place in town. There was one full-service restaurant, but very few people went there. At the Green Front, you could buy a hot dog for five cents and a Coca-Cola for five cents. Vance's friends worked there; and Vance, who now made one dollar a day working at a department store from seven to eleven on Saturdays, could afford an occasional hot dog.

By the midthirties, the Depression was easing up; Roosevelt was a hero. Vance's father shifted from teaching school to becoming one of the first to develop the Federal Building and Loan Association. His office was on the top floor of the tallest four-story building in town. He loved teaching, but ninety dollars per month was not enough to provide the family with a car, home, and food, so, he had to change his work.

Vance, through all of this, does not remember the terrible aspects of the Great Depression; he remembers a happy home. He now realizes what the Depression taught him—don't buy anything you can't pay cash for except a home and car, then pay off the debt on those two items as soon as you can. People learned to appreciate things they owned, not things they were paying on.

Vance later appreciated that the lessons of the courtroom applied to medicine. Physicians collect clues, some are seen directly and some come to them indirectly. Some clues are more diagnostic of an illness than others. But clues may be wrong, just as a witness may say he or she saw a certain man kill another man may be wrong. The diagnostic work of a doctor is an experience in probabilities, just as the work of the lawyer and jury is in many civil and criminal court trials.

13

Compassion and Competence*

Dr. Vance Connelly always believed that the compassion physicians felt for their patients should lead them to think and study, which, in turn, would lead them to become more competent. Simply stated, physicians who care deeply for the welfare of their patients want the best for them, so they struggle to improve their knowledge as well at its delivery.

Dr. Dwight McGoon said it best. Dr. McGoon was a brilliant young cardiac surgeon at the Mayo Clinic, who, at a young age, had to give up surgery because of Parkinson's disease. He wrote:

> How does one take that long walk from the operating room to look into the eyes of a pathetic, frightened, crushed mother to tell her her child is dead or dying of a deformed heart that we couldn't fix, and then squeeze

the father's arm as he struggles to gulp back
a wave of spiritual and physical nausea? Your
compassion for your patients—trying to do the
best for them—must be the major motivating
force in your effort to remain competent.[*]

Vance would read Dr. McGoon's words to medical
students and house officers, hoping their magic would
lead them to understand what real doctoring is all
about.

---

[*]   Permission to quote Dr. McGoon was given to the author
by Mrs. McGoon.

14

A Red Nose

Why was his nose so red? Several doctors, all friends and neighbors of the man with the red nose, had gathered in his home because the man's wife had called them.

A few minutes before the scene described above took place, Dr. Vance Connelly was talking with his wife, Jennifer. The stinging ring of the telephone interrupted Jennifer's sentence. Vance placed the receiver to his ear and said half a hello. The obviously excited lady on the phone said, "He has cardiac arrest. This is June. Harry had cardiac arrest. I tried to blow in his mouth, but air won't go through."

Vance knew Harry. He was an extremely capable endocrinologist and a problem solver of the highest order. As an administrator, he could calmly and slowly extract what he wanted from the most stubborn adversary. He was called Iron Pants because of his extraordinary talent. He had an arteriovenous malformation in the brain and had an occasional seizure. He handled the constant threat with apparent calmness. Vance suspected that Harry had had a seizure but was alarmed when June said the air she blew in him with her mouth-to-mouth breathing would not make his chest move. Harry said, "Blow in his nose, pull his jaw up and back, and blow."

She did so. He began to respond. She said on the phone, "It's working."

Vance responded, "I am on my way."

Vance lived about fifteen minutes away. He broke the speed limit; he held his stethoscope out the window to signal to the cops that his speeding was due to an emergency.

When he arrived, Harry was sitting in a chair; June was at his side, and several doctor friends were talking with each other. One of them said, "June did a great job. Harry seems to be fine, just a little confused. But why is his nose so red?"

Vance, examining Harry's nose, said, "It looks like lipstick. June was having trouble with mouth-to-mouth resuscitation. I advised her to use his nose—it's her lipstick!" All the doctors had a big laugh, and Harry, as usual, wondered what the fuss was all about.

15

Be a Long-Range Rebel[*]

There are two kinds of rebels. One is the "instant rebel," and the other is the "long-range rebel."

The instant rebel sees what he believes is wrong and points it out. He uses many methods. Unfortunately, such a rebel frequently points out what is generally known. He may not offer a solution to the problem. He may assume a proud posture because he feels he has done something. Such a rebel may shift from cause to cause, but he rarely works for a solution to the problems associated with the cause. In fact, he may not persist in his rebellion. He may even become the most apathetic among us. Such a rebel has learned that is it easy to join

---

[*] Reprinted from J. Willis Hurst, *Four Hats* (Chicago: Year Book Medical Publishers, Inc. 1979), 50-51. The author owns the copyright.

with other rebels and to fight an obvious establishment. He has not learned that it is difficult to fight alone and to confront an elusive establishment.

There is another kind of rebel, the long-range variety. He is more likely to identify problems and to work toward solving them. Such a rebel may be fighting problems on many sides. He learns to be effective in his efforts and, furthermore, to remain effective. He learns how to push first in one area and then in another. He recognizes that it is not always proper to use a bulldozer to push people aside. He makes a certain amount of reasonable progress in one problem area and then senses he has gone far enough for the moment. He moves to another problem but returns to the first problem at a later time. He is dedicated to being a rebel as long as he lives. He can fight alone if need be. He can work in the midst of an archaic establishment if the task requires it. He can influence the members of the establishment to raise their sights. The job is not easy, but he does it.

The instant rebel screams, "Why doesn't someone do something about the poor medical care in the hospitals, nursing homes, and doctors' offices?" Having screamed, he may then enter a field that forever removes him from the unpleasant scene. The long-range rebel proclaims, "The medical care in the hospitals, nursing homes, and doctors' offices is inadequate!" He then says, "Come join me in improving it. Let us start with improving our knowledge, creating new ways of bringing patients, doctors, nurses, and others together. Let us lead the public to understand that the source and support of personnel is the public itself."

Maybe we need both kinds of rebels. Who knows? One thing is certain, we will always have both kinds.

16

Attitudes about Education[*]

It is not uncommon for entering students to view the university or the medical school as a place where things are done for them. They may feel that since they pay for their education (or think they do), it is the school's responsibility to assure them that they get one. Some students may even expect the school to schedule the lecture of the visiting Nobel Prize winner at an hour convenient for them rather than for the Nobel Prize winner. If the school does not do so, the students may not attend the lecture. By such an act, the students win—they think. Very curious thinking!

---

[*] Reprinted from J. Willis Hurst, *Four Hats* (Chicago: Year Book Medical Publishers, Inc., 1970), 68-69. The author owns the copyright.

A good university or medical school accepts the fact that many students have the attitude expressed above. An excellent university or medical school sets about leading such students to another view. A school succeeds when the graduates recognize that they must assume the full responsibility for the education of their own brain. The graduate should be determined to explore all aspects of the problems that will become theirs. They realize that there is no shortcut to learning and buckle down to do what must be done to continue their education. Furthermore, if they have been led well, they should be excited about the adventure in personal development, which they can have for the rest of their lives. Such students have learned an approach to learning and will not blame the university or medical school for any of their own shortcomings.

The views expressed by John Gardner are pertinent. He wrote:

> The schools and colleges must equip the student for a never-ending process of learning; they must gird his mind and spirit for the constant reshaping and reexamination of himself. They cannot content themselves with the time-honored process of stuffing students like sausages or even the possibly

more acceptable process of training them like
seals.[1]

Students and faculty should understand these views
and should get on with their jobs.

---

[1]   John W. Gardner, *No Easy Victories* (New York: Harper &
Row Publishers, 1968), 99.

17

The Curriculum and the Establishment*

Medical students voice strong views about the curriculum of the medical school. Superb! House officers also voice their views regarding their medical curriculum. Excellent! On the other hand, the finishing resident seldom plans his own lifelong educational curriculum. Devastating! The students and house officers should be concerned about the curriculum to which they are exposed during their formative years, but they should be even more concerned about the curriculum they develop for themselves for the rest of their lives. Each student and each house officer must realize that his or her future performance

---

* Reprinted from J. Willis Hurst, *Four Hats* (Chicago: Year Book Medical Publishers, Inc., 1970), 100. The author owns the copyright.

depends upon his becoming a self-appointed, one-man curriculum committee with an appointment for life. Each student and house officer must be led to accept his or her role as chairman of his or her own long-term curriculum committee. If students and house officers do not do this, then the concern they have voiced earlier will vanish into pleasant memories, and they will be firmly entrenched in the welcoming arms of a comfortable, nonchanging establishment.

18

To a Son Entering Medical School*

You are about to participate in the most exciting activity of your life. I will watch your development, at a distance. The world of medicine belongs to the young, and you must explore it, alone. The advice I give to you now will be, and must be, near the last that I offer.

You must live each day to the fullest and learn everything around you. Remember that neither your teachers nor the disciplines they teach, be it "basic science" or "clinical medicine," are on trial, you are! Realize that you must learn each discipline for its own value, but more than that, you must translate the

---

* Reprinted from J. Willis Hurst, *Four Hats* (Chicago: Year Book Medical Publishers, Inc., 1970), 39. The author owns the copyright.

** Written September 2, 1967.

information learned in one discipline over to another discipline when it is appropriate.

Scientific "facts" must be learned. This is obvious, and for you, this will be easy. Scientific thought and concepts are more difficult to learn. These must be mastered since this separates the doctor of medicine from the chiropractor.

Learn all you can about yourself. How do you react to the new stimuli? Learn all you can about all kinds of people. How do they react to stimuli? This will lead eventually to an understanding of yourself and an understanding of others.

To succeed, to really succeed, in medicine, you must first be a fine human being who cares about his fellowman, and then you must master scientific concepts.

Good luck! I hope you will find as much excitement and happiness in your life in medicine as I have.

19

A School and a Teacher[*]

The following essay was written by Vance Connelly's father. He was a high school teacher and principal. He was self-made, having started teaching at the age of sixteen in the mountainous area of Kentucky. At the time this essay was written, the Great Depression of the thirties was in full force, and he was living and teaching in a small village in Georgia. For five years, he worked for a new school building, first to sell the concept and then to see that it was erected. The obstacles were great. The residents of the village had been polarized into two camps—a camp that favored the development, and a camp that opposed it. The school was built. New

---

[*] Reprinted from J. Willis Hurst, *Four Hats* (Chicago: Year Book Medical Publishers, Inc., 1970), 3-6. The author owns the copyright.

faculty came. The citizens of the village were proud. Within a few years, the polarization was eliminated, and the school was running smoothly. It was then that he stood up to present his farewell address. The hour was charged with emotion as he spoke.

I am not going so far from you or going to stay away so long as to make the shedding of tears in order. My going is more like that of the tenant farmer who moves over to the next farm. I will still be your neighbor and still be engaged in work that is of mutual interest to us all.

Looking back over the years of my sojourn here and taking a mental review of my efforts and of my "ups and downs" as it were, I find recorded upon the pages of memory so many joys, so many bright spots to remember that they dance continuously before my mind's eye. So I will not dwell upon the less-happy memories. I find myself forgetting the little thorns that have sprung up along the way. Just as the fragile plant called by the children Go-to-Sleep shrinks and closes its petals at human touch, so at the touch of the magic wand of happy memories, the less-happy ones shrink out of sight.

I am convinced that when one has spent any given period of time in an honest effort to discharge to the best of his ability the duties that have come before him, he always comes to the parting of the ways with a feeling of calm resignation, which is worth everything in the world. My friends, I am reveling in that attitude of mind tonight.

I leave you with love and goodwill in my heart, and I turn my face cheerfully toward the task of construction in other communities. I trust you will pardon me if I say, not without a feeling of pride, that I go happy in the knowledge that I leave you in better condition—speaking for an educational point—than I found you. I freely submit, however, that the construction program, which it has been my happy privilege to put over to a certain extent, was not done by me alone. I would give honor and credit and grateful praise to the board of education, the parents and teachers association, and my faithful coworkers, the fine staff of teachers who have labored with me and some of whom will remain to do you further service. I thank my pupils, God bless them all, who have come and learned their lessons and have passed out into the world of social and financial activities. I thank the pastors of our churches who have come and prayed within these walls and have lifted up their voices in prayer for the success of the schoolwork. I thank you all for each and every power and influence that has been exerted for the uplift and ongoing of the cause for which I have labored here. I stand to publicly call you blessed. If there be any who have sponsored destruction rather than construction, I would forget it. I hope you will forget it. I trust that God will not forget them. Life is too short, and time is too precious to indulge in unhappy memories.

Tonight I am too full of the joy of past achievements and of the visions I have of future service to humanity to be able to bring into mental review all that I would like to speak of at this time. I am happy to see my successor with us tonight. Sir, I turn over to you with the best of good wishes one of the best educational plants in existence, one that no matter where I may go or where destiny may lead me will always be enshrined within my heart as mine. Just as the little child looks up into the spacious firmament of heaven and sees a particular star, which by reason and discovery, it claims as its own, so this school will ever be enshrined in my heart as mine, and no accident or incident of future experience can change that feeling within my heart.

There are a few staunch friends and loyal supporters of your school here of whom the entire community should be proud. I would like to call their names, but perhaps I ought not to consume so much time. There is one person, however, who must be identified. He is my good old friend, our village physician. He has been like a father to me. I know that where I am going, I will find good friends, but I will miss this one. I will miss the sight of his honest face each day.

To those boys and girls with whom I have been associated during the past eight years, I wish to say that no matter where you may be in the world and that no matter where I may be, if you should ever need any service that lies in my power to render, do not hesitate to call upon me. Remember I am your friend.

20

Charley[*]

Charley sat in his chair near the window of the nursing home. He sat under a photograph of the parents of the owners of the home. It was one of those old-fashioned types of photographs, you could tell they were good people. He always sat there. Charley had no front teeth. The teeth that were visible through his grin were rusty and worn with age. He wore a brown plaid hat that sported several brightly colored feathers. He kept the brim of the hat rolled up a bit, all the way around. He had an artificial leg on the left. He had lost his leg in a wreck. Charley was a black

---

[*] This essay is reproduced and slightly altered from J. W. Hurst, *Notes From a Chairman—Charley* (Chicago: Year Book Medical Publishers, Inc., 1987), 299-300. The author owns the copyright.

man in a nursing home of whites. Vance's mother was a resident there.

When one walks in a nursing home, one has many thoughts. First of all, the homes have an odor. This is because it is never possible to keep the floors and people clean. Body excrement has its distinct odor that defies masking with air fresheners or perfume. The sense of smell is an interesting sense. One never forgets an odor. Smell something once, and one is likely to remember it forever. So as one walks down the hall of a nursing home, the nose reminds one of the human misery that is there. As you walk farther, you feel profound guilt for being unable to take care of your mother or father some other way. You sense that someday you too may be there. You pass several elderly patients as you make your way to the room where your parent is "living." Some of the patients are singing nonsense, some are groaning constantly, some are asleep in their wheelchairs, and some reach out to touch you. They especially reach out to touch little children and pets. The nursing home personnel are serving the needs of these people who have lost their teeth, vision, and hearing. The nurses try, God knows they try. But trying won't replace the brain cells of the people who live there. You walk farther and see several inhabitants packing their bags, proclaiming that they are going home to their mother who has been dead for fifty years. You see family members visiting their parents, knowing that their visit will be forgotten within minutes after they leave.

Charley sat in his chair near the window in the area near the dining room. He calmly surveyed his peers. He did not talk about his own family who rarely visited him. Charley laughed a lot. His whole body would shake when he laughed. Charley's mind was good, or at least it was better than those around him. He would encourage those who constantly talked of leaving. He would tell them what a great place the nursing home was. He kept an eye on those who came to "sit away" the day near the dining room.

On Sundays, members of the local churches came to sing and entertain the patients. Some of the patients would participate, but most would not. Occasionally, a sleeping patient would come to life and sing an old, old hymn she learned as a child. Charley would be there, encouraging others to join in the "merriment."

Vance's grandchildren often accompanied Jennifer and him when they visited his mother. Vance's mother loved little children even though he had to introduce her great-grandchildren to her each time they visited. Charley would entertain the children by permitting them to tap on his artificial leg with a coin. For some reason, the children liked that, and Charley adored seeing them react to the clicking sound.

Charley walked beautifully on his artificial leg as he went directly to a white man with white hair. The man was stooped and thin. He was blind. He was headed for a collision with an elderly lady in a rocking chair. Charley took care of him. He spoke gently to him and led him to the rail on the wall of the hallway. The rail was familiar to the blind man. He smiled. He looked at Charley but could not see him. Charley went back to his seat and continued to survey his charges.

Charley was smiling when Vance walked up to him. This time, Vance did not miss his missing teeth. Vance only saw his character.

One day, Vance went to the nursing home, and Charley was not there; he was in the hospital. The last time Vance saw Charley, after his return from the hospital, he had lost fifty pounds of body weight. He was in his chair, but his spirit was gone.

The next time Vance visited the nursing home, Charley was gone. Vance won't forget him.

21

Coincidence?*

The series of events you are about to read about could not have happened. That is, they could not have happened according to the rules of mathematical probability. But they did happen in November and December 1951.

Dr. Lon Grove called and asked me to see a patient of his in the recovery room. The date was November 15, 1951. He indicated that his patient's blood pressure was low; she was in circulatory shock. Dr. Grove was a highly respected surgeon. He was famous for his medical judgment, technical ability, and kindness. Virtually all patients he operated on did well.

---

* Reprinted, with modifications, from J. Willis Hurst, *Essays From the Heart* (New York: Raven Press, 1995), 52-61. The author owns the copyright.

I went quickly to the recovery room to see Mrs. Ann Morris. She was thirty-five years old. Dr. Grove had removed a portion of her small intestine for what was then called ileitis. The cause of the low blood pressure and shock was not apparent. She was given norepinephrine and intravenous fluid to raise the blood pressure, and after she became stable, she was moved to a private room where private duty nurses were in constant attendance. Her urine output was alarmingly low, and it was obvious she was developing acute renal failure.

Mrs. Morris, with the aid of her husband, remembers the events preceding and immediately after surgery as follows:

"Lord, do with me what You will." This is the prayer I said at the Mass I attended at St. Thomas More Catholic Church on Sunday, a few days before I was scheduled to go into the hospital for major surgery. I had been so ill; I didn't know whether I would live or die. Never in my wildest dreams did I ever think that God really was going to use me as an instrument for a purpose He had in mind.

I have Crohn's disease. Sometimes it is called ileitis or sometimes enteritis. It is a disease of the small intestine, which can cause terrible intermittent pain during its attacks. It is also called a young people's disease, and it came upon me when I was in my twenties. At the time of this surgery, my first, I was thirty-five years old.

At the time, I was making a home for my husband and two small sons—Thomas Jr. who was eight years old, and Gerald who was four. As I was reluctant to leave them, I had gone as long as possible before admitting that something must be done. At the recommendation of a friend, I engaged a very prominent Atlanta surgeon, Dr. Lon Grove. When I saw Dr. Grove for the first time, he ordered X-rays to be taken; and a date was set for surgery. I was admitted to the hospital a few days prior to surgery in an attempt to "build me up."

The surgery took place at approximately 11:00 AM on November 15, 1951. When I awoke in the recovery room, a lady was looking directly at me with apparent distress. At that time, I knew something was wrong. I tried to tell her to please call a Catholic priest to give me the last rites of the church; but to my dismay, I was unable to speak.

I drifted back to sleep and awoke in my room attended by a private nurse. The only thing I remember doing during this period was raising myself up in order to reach into my bedside table drawer to retrieve the religious medal, which I always wore around my neck. I had been asked to remove it before surgery.

I drifted in and out of consciousness for days, it seemed. I had gone into shock, and as a result, my kidneys had shut down. I was attached to a catheter and other tubes; one of which was an oxygen tube going into my nose. This I hated, and I realized that the only person who had the authority to remove it would be Dr. Grove. There were several other doctors who would come in to see me from time to time, but I was too ill to acknowledge them.

Her blood pressure and pulse were stable, but there was less and less urine output. I knew in 1951 to limit fluid intake, especially fluid containing salt, because the kidneys could not excrete it. Accordingly, the administration of intravenous fluid was curtailed drastically. I also knew that the damaged kidney could not excrete potassium, and that a patient's heart would be adversely affected by the retention of potassium. Therefore, I measured the level of serum potassium and observed its effect on the electrocardiogram. I also gave glucose and insulin to lower the level of potassium in the blood.

Despite the precautions and treatment outlined above, the urine output continued to decline, and she developed pulmonary edema. Her serum potassium rose, and the electrocardiogram changed. Mrs. Morris, who had been mentally confused since surgery, became unconscious.

Mrs. Morris needed to be placed on an artificial kidney. She was nearing the point of death. Dr. Arthur Merrill, an Emory University professor of medicine, had been awarded funds for the purchase of an artificial kidney to be located at Grady Memorial Hospital, but it had not yet arrived. It was becoming increasingly apparent, if Mrs. Morris were to live, she would have to be moved to a hospital where an artificial kidney was located.

One day, the electrocardiogram showed dangerous signs of hyperkalemia, and no urine was being produced. I knew there were several artificial kidneys in the country, but my mind was set on Boston. I had finished my cardiology fellowship at the Massachusetts General Hospital only two years earlier and was familiar with the work of Dr. John Merrill at the Peter Bent Brigham Hospital. I called Dr. Merrill and discussed the problem with him. I told Mrs. Morris's husband, Tom, that if she was not better by the next morning, I would take her to Boston. How I would get her there was not evident at the time.

Mrs. Morris, with the aid of her husband, recollects the events as follows:

> Apparently, I was getting worse, and one of the doctors who came into my room with the group, Dr. Willis Hurst, told my husband that if I was no better by the next morning, he would take me to Boston, Massachusetts, to a hospital called Peter Bent Brigham. Dr. Hurst said this hospital had an artificial kidney which could save my life.

The next morning, Mrs. Morris was no better. I knew she would die unless she could make it to Boston. I called the office of Mr. Robert Woodruff, chairman of the board of Coca-Cola and benefactor of Emory University, in hopes that I could obtain the use of the company's private plane. No luck, the plane was in the air somewhere else. I called the airport and eventually reached Eastern Airlines. There were no seats available, and they had no way to transport a critically ill patient. I pleaded. The airline officials weakened and said to come out to the airport because a plane was leaving soon. With this agreement, I called an ambulance and went to Mrs. Morris's room to make the last minute arrangements.

The medical preparations were made. I had already told the administrator of Emory University Hospital of the plan. My colleagues were supportive and encouraging. I had two last minute acts to perform. Neither was accomplished. I wanted to discuss the move again with Mr. Morris, but he was not in his wife's room, and I could not reach him by telephone. I called my wife to tell her I was on the way to Boston; she was out. I then discussed the matter again with Dr. Grove who had seen Mrs. Morris several times a day. As always, he was filled with compassion. He cared so much he said to me with tears in his eyes, "Let me know what it costs, I will take care of it."

I rode in the ambulance with Mrs. Morris and the attendants. We arrived at the old Atlanta airport and were permitted to drive the ambulance up close to the plane. The plane was about to leave. I rushed inside and explained to the ticket agent, who knew nothing about the circumstances, that the plane must not leave without me and my patient. I wrote a personal check for two tickets. I discovered that we would have to change planes in Newark, New Jersey. I made two phone calls. I called my wife who had returned home and asked her to be sure the check was covered. I called my associate, Dr. Bruce Logue, and asked him to make arrangements for an ambulance to be at the Newark airport to assist me in moving Mrs. Morris from one plane to the next.

We moved Mrs. Morris to the plane. The flight attendants asked two passengers to move from their seats on the front right row. I removed the arm rest that separated the seats and, assisted by the ambulance attendants, placed Mrs. Morris's body across the seats. Her head was near the aisle, and her legs touched the floor near the cabin wall. I was permitted to sit on the floor.

We left Atlanta. Mrs. Morris was not conscious. Her lungs were filled with fluid. I planned, if she died, not to alarm the other passengers of this event. I would continue to work with her. Oxygen was continued, and, worrying about hyperkalemia, I had a large syringe filled with glucose and the appropriate amount of insulin to use if needed.

We left Atlanta so abruptly that I had no overcoat, toothbrush, or razor.

We landed in Newark. The ambulance was waiting. The attendants assisted me in moving Mrs. Morris from plane to plane. I remember the cold wind whipping through my pant legs. Except for that, I remember no extraneous events, for all my attention was focused on my patient.

The ambulance was waiting for us in Boston. I recall the trip from the airport to the Peter Bent Brigham as a peaceful ride. I knew then that we would make it.

Dr. Merrill's staff was waiting for us, and within a short time, Mrs. Morris was attached to the artificial kidney. In 1951, the machine was huge and cumbersome to use, but the skilled staff moved with grace and competence.

Mrs. Morris, with the help of her husband, remembers the event as follows:

> I was later told that when we arrived at the Peter Bent Brigham in Boston, I wasn't very pretty. In fact, I was dying. Dr. John Merrill, the head of the dialysis center, was leaving for California the next day. However, he turned me over to three doctors at the hospital who were studying under him. One of these doctors was from New England, another from California, and the third from France.

I was later told that I was immediately attached to the artificial kidney. The artificial kidney was invented by a German doctor only seven years previously. It resembled a big washing machine. An incision was made in my left wrist and a tube attached to the artery in my arm. Another incision was made in my left ankle, and a tube was attached to the vein there. Thereupon, my blood was directed from the arm into the artificial kidney and then back into my body through the ankle. This big washing machine would remove all the impurities from my body, which ordinarily would be removed by the function of my own kidneys. Thereby, my kidneys would be given a rest, in the hope that they would be able to resume their function.

When I awoke, I found the blue-eyed, blond-haired doctor from France beside me. He began to question me. Like a dream, my confused mind went back to World War II, and upon hearing the accent, I thought I was being interrogated on military secrets of which in reality I knew absolutely nothing. I refused to answer. He was really only asking my age, my next of kin, etc.

Mrs. Morris's condition improved after one long run on the artificial kidney. I spent the night in the house officers' quarters. I saw Mrs. Morris the next morning and was stunned; she was, as I recall, eating a specially prepared ice cream cone. She was still confused, but obviously much improved. I began thinking of returning to Atlanta. She remembers:

> It was this same French doctor who noticed the religious medal around my neck, and it was he who called a Catholic priest to give me the last sacraments, which I desired so much when I first came out of surgery. While the priest was administering the sacrament to me, I awoke and found Dr. Hurst there. He was about to leave Boston to return to Atlanta. In the poor state I was in at the time, I failed to thank him.
>
> Several days later I was taken back to the dialysis clinic to have another go on the artificial kidney, and after that, I was taken to a private room. Later I was so happy to see my husband, Tom, arrive at the hospital. A leave of absence had been given to him by his company to be with me for as long as it was necessary. His sister had kindly volunteered to care for our sons.

When I improved somewhat, I was placed in a ward with a number of other women. I liked that very much, as the comings and goings of everyone there helped the time to pass for me.

I was very happy not to have any tubes giving me nutrition, medicine, or oxygen. I did have the catheter, which drained urine into a jug located beside my bed. A few days passed, and I was told that the doctors were considering giving me another treatment on the kidney machine the following day. At the time, I was very anxious to avoid this if possible.

A priest came nightly to visit patients in the ward, and I requested that he please say a Mass for me the next morning; the intention being that if it were possible, I would like to avoid going on the kidney machine a third time. He looked me in the eye and said, "It was the artificial kidney that saved your life." I held up my bandaged arm and said, "Yes, I know, but it is the incisions I am thinking of."

During the night, a nurse I had never seen before came to my bedside and pressed gently on my lower right side. The next morning, the doctors came. They looked at the jug attached

to the catheter, scratched their heads, and left.
My kidney had begun to work! Soon after, I
was brought my breakfast, and I knew that the
procedure had been cancelled. I came to the
conclusion that the nurse who came to my bed
and pressed ever so gently on my side must
have been my guardian angel. My prayers had
been answered!

Back at Emory, I remained in contact with the
physicians at the Peter Bent Brigham Hospital. One
day, one of the physicians called to say they had
discovered an infiltrate in the chest X-ray film of Mrs.
Morris. He asked me to check with the pathologist
who examined the specimen of the small intestine
if there was any evidence of tuberculosis. I checked.
There was no evidence of tuberculosis. I believe I sent
a microscopic slide from Emory University Hospital to
the Brigham so the pathologist there could also review
the slide. Still, the physicians were concerned that the
infiltrate on the chest X-ray film might be caused by
tuberculosis.

Mrs. Morris's kidney function gradually improved,
and she gained strength daily.

Mrs. Morris remembers the events as follows:

While at Peter Bent Brigham, I underwent many tests at doctor's orders. Dr. Hurst had been keeping in touch from Atlanta by telephone to the doctors there. Peter Bent Brigham is one of the teaching hospitals of Harvard Medical School; and one day, I was wheeled into Harvard's surgical theater where I was placed before the doctors of Boston, and my case was reviewed. Another time, I was taken before the navy doctors of Boston where my story was also told.

I was weighed every morning and given a special dietitian who prepared three meals of my favorite foods every day. Often I was given steak with baked potato, along with luscious fattening dessert. I began to gain weight and reached the point of eighty-seven pounds. One nurse rinsed out my gowns. Another gave me a much-needed shampoo. Another went out and bought cosmetics for me. I had nothing at the time. Everyone was so nice to me.

Days passed. Christmas was approaching. Mrs. Morris was improving. Plans were made for Mrs. Morris to return to Atlanta. I planned to admit her to Emory

University Hospital for a few days in order to establish a baseline measurement on her kidneys and heart and to evaluate her lungs.

Mrs. Morris remembers the events as follows:

> Shortly before Christmas, my husband and I received a letter from our brother-in-law stating that our son, Thomas, was very downcast for fear that Santa Claus would pass him and his brother over on Christmas Eve because his parents were not there. I told the doctors that I must go home. I was walking around the ward and was gaining strength.
>
> My husband went to the airline ticket office to purchase the plane tickets and was informed that because of the Christmas holidays, there were no tickets available. Frustrated, he went to the doctors and told them of our plight. They suggested that perhaps if newspaper reporters were called, and if my unusual story was given to the press, that someone might offer us tickets. In addition, the publicity might bring to the forefront the fact that there was a need for an artificial kidney in Atlanta. We were given tickets to Atlanta, and as I left Peter Bent Brigham, I must admit I shed a few tears.

Mrs. Morris arrived in Atlanta a few days before Christmas in 1951. Newspaper reports and photographers were there to cover her arrival home. An ambulance was waiting for her, and she was admitted to Emory University Hospital.

Mrs. Morris remembers the events as follows:

> We arrived in Atlanta and were met at the airport by our sons, family, and friends. An ambulance was waiting to take us to Emory University Hospital where Dr. Hurst pronounced me in good condition, and it wasn't long before I was in my own home.

I reviewed the new X-ray film of the chest with one of our radiologists. I concluded the infiltrate was due to a resolving pulmonary infarction. There was the possibility that Mrs. Morris's original trouble, her shocklike state after abdominal surgery, was due to a blood clot to the lung. This could not be stated with certainty, but the possibility was there. On the other hand, the blood clot could have occurred days later while she was recovering at the Brigham Hospital.

Although Emory professor Dr. Arthur Merrill had already placed an order for an artificial kidney when I transported Mrs. Morris to Boston, the publicity surrounding the trip undoubtedly stimulated even greater interest in developing a renal dialysis unit at Grady Memorial Hospital and Emory University Hospital. In fact, because of the publicity surrounding Mrs. Morris's trip, Drs. Francis Fitzhugh and Ivan Bennett transported a Grady Memorial Hospital patient to the Brigham Hospital during the month of December, 1951. The first kidney dialysis was performed by Emory University staff at Grady Hospital in 1952.

Mrs. Morris visited my wife, Nelie, at Emory University Hospital in 1952. Nelie was in the hospital following the birth of our youngest son. Mrs. Morris, who had not met my wife previously, proclaimed to her, "I thought you should meet the woman your husband took to Boston!"

I have received a Christmas card from Mrs. Morris and her husband each year for forty-two years. The thank-you note is greatly appreciated. I also had lunch at her home, her biscuits were wonderful.

Mrs. Morris completes her story as follows:

> I was under Dr. Hurst's care for several years. Dr. Lon Grove, the surgeon who performed the surgery on that day of November 15, 1951, felt very badly concerning the complications that arose. The surgery itself was a success,

but he deeply regretted the turn of events. In fact, he offered to reimburse my husband for all the expenses that were incurred, and we never received a bill from him.

As the doctors in Boston predicted, the newspapers in Atlanta picked up my story from the Boston papers. The publicity stimulated further interest in the development of an artificial kidney at Emory University and Grady Memorial Hospital.

Since 1951, the artificial kidney has been improved and perfected. Instead of being a big washing machine, it is small and very sophisticated, with a permanent device to enter the arm and leg, rather than a fresh incision to be made each time. Now, of course, there are many throughout Atlanta and the entire nation.

More than forty-two years have passed since that dark November day of 1951. As was always my wish, I was able to raise my sons myself. Our eldest son, Thomas Jr., is a theoretical physicist doing research in Huntsville, Alabama. Our youngest son, Gerald, is a mortgage banker in Atlanta. My husband and I celebrated our fiftieth wedding anniversary six years ago.

Crohn's disease has a tendency to return, and during the years, I have had to undergo two more surgeries. However, these were routine with no problems. I am seventy-seven years of age and have had a very happy life. I thank Dr. Hurst each year at Christmastime, which marks the anniversary of our trip.

It is my belief that God heard and acted on the prayer I made on that Sunday at St. Thomas More Catholic Church. I believe He used me to stimulate additional interest in the development of Emory University's kidney program at Grady Memorial Hospital.

The laws of mathematical probability used in scientific medicine rule against the likelihood of a successful outcome for a patient such as Mrs. Morris. So, was her survival a *coincidence* or the influence of *Christmas*?

I occasionally tell this story to medical students and house officers. I ask them, "How much should I have charged her?" They respond as I hoped they would, with a resounding "nothing." Being satisfied with the answer, I point out, with a little moisture in my eyes, "Yes, yes, to send a bill would ruin the entire event."

PS: Mrs. Morris lived until 2005, fifty-four years after her trip to Boston. The obituary prepared by her children included a lengthy discussion of her trip to Boston in 1951. I have used my name in this story because part of the story is written by Mrs. Morris, and she uses my real name.

22

The Future Is Yours, but Not Merely

to Hold*

You, who are graduating from the Medical College of Georgia in 1971, will change. This will occur for two reasons. First, there are forces which are external to you which will produce changes. Secondly, your internal reactions to the external forces will change. I wish to present to you a few comments regarding the external

---

* Reprinted from J. Willis Hurst, *Essays From the Heart* (New York: Raven Press, 1995), 13-19. The author owns the copyright.

** This essay was presented by Vance Connelly to the graduates of the Medical College of Georgia in Augusta, Georgia, on June 5, 1971. Vance's son was one of the graduates.

changes that are to affect you as a member of the health profession and to suggest to you some of the internal changes that you may consider for yourself.

Five Dangers to Avoid

I recently received a telegram from Senator Ted Kennedy. It arrived at 1:00 PM, Saturday. He indicated he wanted seventy-five copies of a prepared statement that I would present to his subcommittee on health. He furthermore indicated he wanted the material by Monday morning. The following material was written and mailed to him. The statement was actually presented to Senator Kennedy's subcommittee the following Tuesday, April 6, 1971.

Dangers await us unless the following concepts are considered as we attempt to solve the health care crisis.

The either-or question

The popular technique of asking one to choose between two possible solutions to a problem may, at times, be dangerous. The proper answer may not be either of the solutions offered but may be something else. The *Peanuts* cartoon by Charles Schulz makes the point. Lucy is seen in her stand playing the part of a psychiatrist. She asks Charlie Brown the following question: "Do you prefer sunrise or sunset?" Charlie answers, "Sunset, I suppose." Lucy then responds by saying, "People who prefer sunset are dreamers! They always give up! They always look back instead of forward! Sunrisers are go-getters! They have ambition and drive! Give me a person who likes a sunrise every time! Yes, sir! I am sorry, Charlie Brown . . . if you prefer sunset to sunrise, I cannot take your case . . . you are hopeless!" Lucy then walks away. Charlie then remarks, "Actually, I have always sort of preferred noon." The design of Lucy's question restricted Charlie's response. The phrasing of some questions being asked today restricts one's response and, in my judgment, prevents a proper answer. For example, we hear that we must choose between the delivery of health care and medical research. This type of statement obscures the correct answer. The correct answer is that we must have both and that we must strive to achieve a proper balance between the two. We are led to believe that we must choose between the quantity of health care and the quality of health care. We are told that we need more general physicians and fewer specialists. While this is true, we also need a system to relate each group to the other. We are led to believe that we must choose between governmental support of medicine and the private support of medicine, when the true answer is that we will need both. The list of such questions and statements is endless. We must not fall into the trap and give a hasty answer when the truth may be in a third option. Voices will be raised to say that many of the third options will cost too much. My response is that it will cost too much not to look at third options. I am convinced that heath care will not be improved in quantity or quality unless all citizens recognize that it will cost a great deal more than it costs now. The voices will say it can't be done. I will say that we must rearrange our priorities of values and that medical care should be at the top.

The pursuit of excellence must continue

I realize that a discussion regarding excellence is not a popular subject, but we must consider it because it is right. When it becomes difficult or nearly impossible to pursue the best, then mediocrity will reign. All Americans must be inspired to give the best that is in them. The fact that a few medical scientists were able to improve the world of medicine, and, in turn, the health of the people, is why we have a health crisis. Their research paid off. That is why we have something to deliver. Since we physicians don't yet know enough, it follows that research must continue in order to have something to deliver. It also follows that we need a more effective delivery system in order to deliver the fruits of research.

The problem may be likened to an arrow. The sharp tip of the arrowhead should be made up of those individuals who choose to do research in the medical problems that plague mankind. The remainder of the arrowhead should be made up of those who spend their lives setting the highest possible standard for patient care. The long arrow shaft should represent the delivery of the bulk of medical care in the country. While the roles played by individuals at the arrow tip, at the remainder of the arrowhead, and at the arrow shaft are different, each must strive for excellence. The arrow will not enter its flight until citizens place it into their financial bow and shoot it into the air. Should all of this be done, then our society will be on its way to solving the health crisis.

We must encourage our talented young people, who will make up our future health personnel. Therefore, the institutions that train them must be supported. The medical students, interns, residents, specialty trainees, nurses, and allied health personnel must be appropriately supported. We cannot leave the risk of training them to chance alone. We must develop a way in ensuring its occurrence, and the training must be excellent.

When you have your heart attack, which you are likely to have, you must have a highly trained physician at your bedside. This does not mean that there should not be far more generalists than specialists. It simply means that we must have both and that we cannot leave the development of either to chance. If you wish to prevent your heart attack, which you are likely to have, then you must support the development of research people to work on the subject, because no one can guarantee you a method of prevention today. A young intern in my program recently diagnosed himself as having leukemia and died within one month. He is on my mind. We need more research to prevent tragedies such as this.

Should excellence in the field of patient care not be held as a national goal, then we will be less than we could be. If excellence in medical care is not to be an objective, then it is likely that excellence will not be sought generally in this country. Should the pursuit of excellence be ignored, the spirit of man will die. The failure to appreciate excellence is dangerous indeed!

Health education is necessary in order to develop a workable health care system

In my opinion, a new health care system will not work unless a health educational system is developed in parallel with it. Without a health education system, the citizens might under use or overuse the new health care system. It takes health knowledge, not just health concern, to use a health care system properly. Accordingly, I urge that health be taught in every grade in school. We must start in the first grade and continue to teach health throughout the individual's student days. After students leave formal school, then a health education system must be available to them for the rest of their lives. The physician's waiting room and the hospital lobby must become educational facilities for the patients who go there. All hospitals must become educational centers for patients, visitors, and for those who work there. Remember, a citizen today should know about as much about health as a physician knew fifty years ago.

Continuing education must become a way of life for physicians and all health care personnel. It is impossible to have good patient care without continuing education for those who deliver the service.

It will be dangerous to underestimate the need for health education for all citizens, including those who deliver the service.

Cost accounting is necessary, but it may be dangerous

We must never forget that human life and comfort are priceless. Whereas it may be necessary to put a dollar figure on health matters in order to have some semblance of order, it is inhumane and uncivilized to carry the concept to the extreme. I plead with all who hear my words not to be an extremist in this regard. Any thoughtful person should recognize that the improvement of heath care will cost many more times than is currently expended. It will be dangerous to underestimate the cost of good medical care for all citizens.

Who shall do the planning?

The planners of a new health care system must involve people other than physicians. No one can doubt that. It will be dangerous, however, to plan without the help of physicians. Accordingly, I urge all health care planners to seek the help of thoughtful physicians to assist them in planning for the future. Not doing so will be a mistake.

Whereas I have stressed some of the dangers I see ahead of us, I wish to emphasize that I am in no way pessimistic about the future. I actually believe we are entering a golden era, an era that will show the profession of medicine serving mankind in its finest way. The dangers are highlighted in order to emphasize that we must have balanced programs. We must develop an approach that considers a proper balance between research, education, and patient care. This is no cliché. It is, I am absolutely certain, the truth. Just as a boat with too much weight at one end capsizes, an unbalanced health care system will sink, and its passengers, the patients, will go down with it. The proper balance between research, education, and patient care must become the common purpose of those who wish to improve the medical care of the citizens.

Now, having delivered my message to Senator Kennedy's subcommittee on health, I wish to speak directly to you. A good university leads its students to realize that they are responsible for the development of their own brains. I suspect that you realize that as you end your years of formal schooling. But there is another kind of schooling. It is the schooling of self-discipline. It is self-discipline that makes one competent. Remember, a great writer like Stevenson wrote and rewrote the sentences that made him a professional. Remember that Toscanini worked and worked until he knew every note in a hundred symphonies. Remember that Joe Frazier worked and worked until he was a champion. But most of all, remember that health workers are professionals who work with human beings. Nothing can be nobler than that. Professional health workers must be competent. They cannot vote their way into the world of the competent. They cannot protest their way into the world of the competent. They cannot wish their way into the world of the competent. They can only enter that world as Stevenson, Toscanini and Frazier entered it, by possessing self-discipline and by working as a professional should.

The health profession is changing rapidly. You must assist in the change. You should retain the old that is good and add the new that is needed. If you do this, the future will be uniquely yours, and in doing so, the world will be better. Should you do this, I urge you to retain the following old views. You must relate properly to your fellowman, and you can't do that professionally if you don't do it generally. You must become very competent in your profession, and you can't do that without self-discipline and work. I dare not tell you what you should create, which is new. That is your responsibility and opportunity. Should I, or someone else, tell you what to create, then it would not be your creation. Let me leave no doubt in your mind. You are to create the new we need. If you do, the future will be yours.

The future is yours, not merely to hold, but to mold. The future is yours, not merely to endure, but to enjoy. You will enjoy it, if you search for, find, and solve problems before the problems find and destroy you. Now as I close, I wish to paraphrase the words of Mac Hyman and say, I hope you find what you are searching for, and after you find it, I hope you still want it.

23

Jeff—an Unforgettable Man[*]

It was 1946. World War II had ended, but the effects of the war were still with us. Vance, Jennifer, and their small son arrived in Denver, where Vance was to begin work as a medical officer at Fitzsimons General Hospital. They could not find a house to rent, so they stayed in motels while they looked for a suitable place to live. The Office of Price Administration had a rule. If you stayed more than nine days at a motel, the management was required to give you monthly rates. So the management simply asked guests to move every nine days and profited by charging the higher daily rates. Vance and Jennifer moved several times but

---

[*] Reprinted from J. Willis Hurst, *Notes From a Chairman* (Chicago: Year Book Medical Publishers, Inc., 1987), 300-303. The author owns the copyright.

resolved not to give up. One day, Jennifer was sunning their young son in a small area outside of a motel on Colfax Avenue when the postman arrived to deliver the mail.

Jeff, the postman, had distinct characteristics, so he is easy to describe. He was about six feet tall. His walk was his and no one else's. He took long steps and seemed to wear oversized shoes. He swayed a little from side to side as he galloped along. With it all, he had a slight limp, caused when a car hit him while he was standing in the middle of the street taking a photograph. He held his head a little to the side when he talked. His hair was cut short above the ears, but was long on top, the front part dropping over his forehead. He had a receding chin that always needed a shave. His glasses were thick, and when you looked through them, his eyes seemed to be very small. Jeff, the postman, stopped to talk with Jennifer and her newfound friend, Jeanie. The conversation went something like this:

"Where are you from?" he asked.

"I am from Georgia, and my friend is from New Jersey."

"How long you been here?" he asked.

"At this place?"

"Yes."

"Three days. We move every nine days."

He pondered a moment and said, "Want to rent a house?"

"Sure," Jennifer answered in an excited voice.

"Well," he said, "I have one to rent. It needs some work on it, and I don't want to rent it to one family. If your husband will finish closing in the kitchen and if you will get another family to join you, it is yours. It's too big for one couple, and I want to help two couples."

Jeanie and her husband were moving on, so Vance and Jennifer had to find another couple. They found Jane and Joe of North Carolina. Joe was also a medical officer at Fitzsimons. They also had a small boy and had no place to live. The house was on Boston Avenue in the middle of the town of Aurora. Boston Avenue made a right-angle turn off Colfax Street. The house was old. It was a wooden structure with a screened-in front porch and was located about twenty feet from the street. The downstairs had a living room, dining room, two bedrooms, kitchen, and a bathroom. The kitchen was really unfinished; its backside had just sort of fallen out. The upstairs had no floor and was unusable. Joe and Vance decided they could fix up the house and finish the kitchen. Jeff offered to furnish all the material needed to make the house livable if Joe and Vance would do all the work. Jeff also delayed the day their rent started for one month. So, the families moved in, and they began to work on the house at night when Vance and Joe got home from the hospital.

Jeff lived in a house only a few feet behind the rental house. He had converted an old goat barn into an attractive home. He lived there with his wife, Mary, and their son, who, unfortunately, had kidney disease.

Jeff had many interests. He was a skilled photographer and seemed to be in demand. He made photographs of Vance and Jennifer and numerous photographs of their son. He would not accept money for the photographic work he did for them. As mentioned earlier, being absentminded, he was hit by a car when he was making a photograph of a street!

Jeff loved bargains. One day, Vance arrived home and encountered a most unusual sight. Jeff was surveying his front yard with pride. Most of the front yard was covered by rolled-up pairs of army socks. He had bought a thousand or so pairs of socks from army surplus. He asked Vance to take a bunch. Vance kidded him by asking, "Do you really believe you can plant socks like you plant corn?" Good-natured Jeff smiled and continued to enjoy surveying his crop of socks. Vance does not know what Jeff did with the socks.

One day, Mary yelled in a shrill voice, "Jeff, Jeff, come here. Get that stuff out of my house. I will take a broom to you."

Jeff came loping down the street and sailed into the front door and then out the back door. He then threw an object into the trash. Then we knew what it was. Vance and Jennifer had given Jeff some very strong-smelling cheese that someone had given them. He wanted it and claimed he loved that type of cheese. Jeff then loped on down the street to continue whatever he was doing.

Joe went to Japan, and Jane and little Joe returned to North Carolina. Vance and Jennifer missed them. Vance and Jennifer paid half of the rent until they found another family to move into the house. Jeff insisted that he wanted to help two families but would not permit Vance and Jennifer to pay all of the rent. They discovered Tom and Helen from Michigan. Tom was also a medical officer at Fitzsimons. They had two children and another on the way. Accordingly, it was necessary to complete the stairs and two rooms upstairs to make sufficient room for them. Tom and Vance did that. Tom was an excellent carpenter. A little later, Tom was sent to Japan, but Jane and their children stayed on. Vance was released from the army a little early because of a tragedy in his wife's family. (But that is another story to be told at a different time.)

Whenever Vance was in Denver, he had a strong pull to return to Boston Avenue in Aurora. Jeff had unforgettable physical and character traits. He was a friend when Vance and Jennifer needed a friend. As Vance looks back, he is pleased with the adaptability he and Jennifer demonstrated. It was where their first son took his first step. It was where their son had his first haircut by a barber. It was where they bought their first new car. It was where they tried to raise a vegetable garden. It was where they made lasting friendships. Tom and Helen moved to Hawaii, and Vance and Jennifer visited them often on their trips there. What do they talk about? Jeff, of course.

There was only one Jeff.

24

Old Teachers Never Die

When Vance discontinued teaching at Greystone University Hospital on January 1, 2009, the interns and residents he taught wanted to visit Vance so he could continue teaching them. Vance considered their request to be the finest compliment of his career, so he jumped at the chance to be with them. He reserved Brookland's *Private Dining Room* the first Tuesday of each month for dinner and a teaching session. Vance discussed many topics, tried to answer many questions, and encouraged the interns to think, write clearly, and speak coherently, attributes of good doctoring that were gradually slipping away.

One Tuesday night, Vance invited an eighty-year-old woman to the meeting to tell of her experience with her husband who had died thirteen years earlier. She, being uncommonly smart and confident in her talk, told a story that Vance wanted the young doctors (still in training) to hear.

She said, "My husband was in and out of the hospital. He had heart failure."

Vance gently interrupted and asked, "Were you satisfied with the treatment?"

"No," she responded.

"What happened?" Vance asked.

"Even though he was in and out of the hospital, at times, he was in the cardiac care unit, the doctor only talked to me one time and that was on the phone!"

Vance interrupted again and asked, "You went to the hospital, you were there, but your doctor did not talk to you?"

"That's right."

"Did the interns and residents talk to you?"

"No. My life, and my husband's life, would have been better if they had."

Vance said, with obvious sadness in his voice, "Thank you for sharing your story. I wanted my friends to hear you. I know they will never forget it. You see, I try, I try to tell them that good doctors communicate with their patients and their patients' families. In fact, patients judge their doctor on things they understand, such as kindness and caring. They trust that their doctors know what they are doing. You must never let them down. Good doctors feel incomplete if they do not sit and talk with their patients and their families. Thank you for coming."

"It was my pleasure," she said. "I hope it helped. Just remember please, patients and their families need you, and you must never forget that you need them, so be nice to them."

After she left, Vance asked the group of eight nascent young doctors, "Do you get the message?"

25

A Modern-Day Charles Dickens[*]

The following article appeared in the *Savannah Morning News* on December 2, 1958. The author was Patrick Kelly, in whom Charles Dickens has a keen competitor.

THE SAVANNAH MORNING NEWS
Tuesday, December 2, 1958

RARE PICKWICKIAN SYNDROME
DELAYS BELLINGER HEARING

---

[*] Reprinted from J. Willis Hurst, *Disconnected Odds and Ends of Cardiology, Transactions of the American Clinical and Climatological Association* (1961), 160-161. Used with permission.

By patrick kelly
Morning News Staff

Sloppy Joe Bellinger, Savannah's alleged boledo king, will not stand trial in City Court today.

The fabulous 425-pound Bellinger, arrested in a fabulous raid by city detectives last month, has a fabulous ailment, which, apparently, will prevent his appearance in any court for a fabulous length of time.

The illness is something straight from the classics—Pickwickian syndrome. It is certified as the proper diagnosis of Bellinger's case not only by the patient's doctor, but by an impartial physician appointed by the court to look into the situation. The Pickwickian syndrome is a condition sometimes encountered in obese individuals. They have a strong tendency to fall asleep quite involuntarily—specially when under stress.

Bellinger's attorney, Ralph L. Crawford, first noticed his client's affliction when he tried to consult with him about his defense in the boledo case scheduled for jury trial today.

"He would doze off right in the middle of a sentence—er, let's say phrase," Crawford declared. He called in a doctor. The doctor shook his head.

"Pickwickian syndrome," he said, "very interesting, indeed."

Crawford telephoned Chief Asst. Sol. Gen. Sylvan A. Garfunkel.

"I cannot prepare my defense in the Bellinger case," he said. "My client has a Pickwickian syndrome."

"Very interesting," replied Garfunkel. "I'll tell the judge."

"Very interesting," observed Judge Columbus E. Alexander when so informed. "Have another physician examine Bellinger."

Accordingly, another doctor was commissioned to perform the task.

"Very interesting, indeed," he said, shaking his head as he completed it, "Pickwickian syndrome."

"Isn't there any way he can be brought to trial?" inquired Garfunkel, unhappily. "After all, the solicitor general's office asked for the case after it had been turned over to the federal government."

"Yes," the physician replied, "he could be tried if he were kept on his feet and moving around constantly. If you try to put him in the witness chair, he'll fall asleep. And if he were convicted, you probably couldn't put him in jail in his condition."

"We have no choice then but to pass the case until the next term of court," decided Garfunkel. "Will the patient improve?"

"He might improve if he diets stringently," the doctor declared. "It's a condition brought about by being overweight."

A telephone call to Bellinger's home Monday night did not elicit much hope.

"Joe's sleeping," the voice on the other end of the line said, "he had an extra big supper tonight."

This story of Sloppy Joe Bellinger illustrates some of the physiological and psychological problems in some fat people. This is the only case report in the literature that illustrates the total disruption of a court of law by a defendant who has the "Pickwickian syndrome."

26

A Threat*

Dr. Vance Connelly was sitting at his desk reviewing a manuscript that he hoped would be accepted in a peer review medical journal, when the loud ring of the telephone startled him.

"Hello, is this Dr. Vance Connelly?" The caller was a lady. She talked very nice and was obviously very skilled at talking on the phone.

"Just a second, Dr. Connelly," she cooed.

After a second, a man came on the phone, he was the very opposite to the nice, cooing lady. He uttered, "I mean business. You must pay up. I will call later and instruct you." He then hung up.

---

* Reproduced, with modifications, from J. W. Hurst, *The Quest of Excellence* (Georgia: Scholars Press, 1997), 30-37. Reproduced with permission.

Vance was stunned. He tried to think, *What is that all about?*

Vance left his desk to talk with his administrative assistant. He told him, "I have just been threatened—it's not clear what this is about—I have received hostile calls before because I am the physician to the president, but none have been threatening. He will call again, I wanted you to know."

A few days later, the man called again. The sweet-talking lady introduced him again. This time, he talked even rougher. He said, "Are you ready to pay? If you are not, I must tell you I know where your mother lives. I will get her." He then hung up.

Vance was reeling in the reality that he was being threatened, but he did not know why. He called Jennifer and asked her to be very careful with the three boys. He called his mother who lived in a small town, Vance's hometown, fifty miles from Atlanta. He told her that she might get a call from some bad people or they might show up at her front door. As expected, the news did not bother her; she was an individualist who could take care of herself. Vance called the sheriff who lived across the street from his mother and said, after explaining the situation, "Please take care of my mother."

The sheriff answered, "Vance, you know I will do that."

Still, Vance did not understand what was going on. He received a third call from the rough-talking man who said, "Next time I call, I will tell you where to meet me with the money." He hung up without saying how much money or for what.

Vance then called the Atlanta police. He also called Tommy who was in the FBI. Tommy was an old friend and former college roommate. Vance also called Jerry who had been in the Secret Service and traveled with the president. Vance knew him because he also traveled with the president.

A day or so later, Vance got a call from the Atlanta police who said, "We have your man." Apparently, Tommy, the smart FBI man, had solved the case. Tommy had asked Vance what he remembered about the first call. Vance answered, "This sweet-talking lady who always preceded the tough-talking man would say a few nice things before he lowered the boom."

"Do you remember anything she said?"

Vance vaguely remembered that on the first call, she said something like Seville, but he was not sure.

Tommy knew a shop named Seville. He went there and sized up the place; he pretended he was buying a hat. This led him to questioning the clerk about their charging policy. Somehow, this eventually led to the revelation of their policy to turn delinquent payments over to a collection agency. In fact, they had an example to show him. "Dr. Vance Connelly," the clerk said, "wrote a check to pay for a pair of shoes. The check bounced, and we turned the collection over to a very fine collection agency."

The collection agency used severe and rough tactics to scare the daylight out of the person they were to shake down.

It turned out a person had written a check to pay for a pair of shoes and had forged Vance Connelly's name on the check. The police knew him and captured him promptly. The collection service obviously did not realize that the name on the check was forged.

Vance was greatly relieved when he learned that the culprit had been arrested.

27

What Is the Definition of a Profession?

The word *profession* is poorly understood. Dr. Vance Connelly often asked young medical students, interns, residents, and fellows the following question: "Since you are working hard to be a member of the medical profession, what is your definition of a profession?"

Dead silence was the usual response. This was a bit bewildering to Vance. No one had ever asked them such a question, and they had not asked themselves such a question. Vance usually broke the silence by asking two more questions. He asked, "Is wrestling a profession? When a person makes a living wrestling or boxing, the word *professional* is applied to their work. Is that the correct use of the word?"

Vance would usually leave the discussion at that point but would challenge the trainees to "think about it, argue about the answer, and be prepared to answer the questions tomorrow."

Then, without fail, when tomorrow came, Vance reopened the question. Their answers were much improved after their very capable brains attacked the problem.

Vance would usually submit the following to them to think about: "In the beginning, there were five professions: teaching, medicine, the law, the military, and the ministry. Note that those who participated in these acts were delivering services. They had no product to sell. They all received their emotional kicks from the service they delivered. They all were participants in work that was for the public good. They all created a trusting relationship with those they served. As time passed, the profession established rules for training and performance and became self-regulating, that is, hiring, firing, and disciplinary actions were carried out by the profession." Vance pointed out that certain types of farming and entertainment might also be labeled as professions.

"So," Vance would continue, "you and I are faced with this problem. How does one make a living, gain access to money, in a profession that by definition must serve those who need their skill even when no money is available? The excellent teacher makes this point. They teach even though their financial income is small. The minister preaches without much thought of money. In medicine, we face another problem that is highlighted when one asks, 'What is an eye worth?' The businessman, the CEO, does not face such questions. The answer, of course, is that the value of the eye is priceless. So how do you place a price on the value of the work a physician does to save the eye or a life? The work done is either priceless or worthless."

Judge Elbert Tuttle answered these questions in a 1957 graduation address at Greystone University. Vance was beginning his first year as chairman of the department of medicine. The speech became the motto of his developing department, and, for more than fifty years, he shared the view with anyone who would listen. Tuttle said and wrote:

> The professional man is in essence one who provides services. But the service he renders is something more than that of the laborer, even the skilled laborer. It is a service that wells up from the entire complex of his personality. True, some specialized and highly developed techniques may be included, but their mode of expression is given its deepest meaning by the personality of the practitioner. In a very real sense, his professional service cannot be separate from his personal being. He has no

goods to sell, no land to till; his only asset is himself. It turns out that there is no right price for service, for what is a share of a man worth? If he does not contain the quality of integrity, he is worthless. If he does, he is priceless. The value is either nothing or it is infinite.

So do not try to set a price on yourselves. Do not measure out your professional services on an apothecary's scale and say, "Only this for so much." Do not debase yourselves by equating your souls to what they will bring in the market. Do not be a miser, hoarding your talents and abilities and knowledge, either among yourselves or in your dealings with your clients, patients, or flock. Rather, be reckless and spendthrift, pouring out your talent to all, to whom it can be of service! Throw it away, waste it; and in the spending, it can be of service. Do not keep a watchful eye, lest you slip, and give away a little bit of what you might have sold. Do not censor your thoughts to gain a wiser audience. Like love, talent is useful only in its expenditure, and it is never exhausted. Certain it is that man must eat, so set what price you must on your service. But never confuse the performance, which is

great, with the compensation—be it money,
power, or fame, which is trivial.*

Vance would ask the trainees again after the
discussion, including the Tuttle definition: "Is wrestling
or boxing a profession? No, of course not. They serve
no public good. Is the CEO of a company who makes
twenty million dollars a year even when the company
fails, who spends millions of company money on a
lavish lifestyle, spending more than eight thousand
company dollars on a rug for his office and almost
fifteen hundred dollars for a commode, a professional
person, meeting all the attributes of a professional as
described earlier in this essay?"

Members in a profession can act nonprofessionally.
Should they do so, the members of the profession must
stop it. Faking the numbers in a clinical trial, taking
money from a pharmaceutical house to "sell" their
drugs by prescribing them is not professional.

The medical dilemma of the present, and the
future, is the following: How does the profession of

---

* Reprinted from J. Willis Hurst, *Four Hats* (Chicago: Year
Book Medical Publishers, Inc., 1979), 34-35. The author
owns the copyright.

medicine continue when the cost of modern medical care now involves the use of expensive medications and procedures? The good doctors can give their services away, but they can't give away the expensive medications and procedures. They can, however, be certain that the medications and procedures that are so expensive are really needed for the care of the patient. Accordingly, good doctors must be able to separate the *hype* from the *truth*.

28

A Call on New Year's Day

In the seventies, almost forty years ago, Dr. Vance Connelly received a telephone call from two friends in Washington, D.C. The hour of the call was about 8:00 PM.

"Vance," the caller said, "we want you to fly to Miami to consult on a dear friend of ours."

Vance responded, "Tell me more. Does his doctor there request the consult?"

"Oh yes," they answered. "He wants you to come. Our friend has some sort of blood vessel catastrophe, and they fear he will die. Will you please go see him?"

"Yes, of course. I will catch the next plane."

When Vance arrived at the Miami airport at 2:00 AM, he was met by a rabbi. After identifying each other, the rabbi drove Vance to the hospital to see the patient. They talked on the way. The rabbi, a small man with a rather typical beard, was obviously highly intelligent and was a very caring individual. He had flown down from New York to be with his sick friend.

Vance examined the patient. He hated to inform the patient's family and the rabbi what he had discovered. The patient had a condition known as dissection of the aorta, the middle layer of the aorta and many other arteries had given way. At times, surgical intervention can save the patient, but not in this case. The damage was too extensive. Vance agreed that the doctors there were delivering the best medicine that is known for such a terrible problem.

After discussing the patient's condition with the family, Vance was driven back to the Miami airport by the rabbi who thanked him profusely for making the trip.

Time passed. New Year's Day arrived. Vance was at home. He answered the phone. A man said, "This is your rabbi friend." The rabbi talked rapidly; every word counted: "how are you," "I won't forget you for coming to Miami"—a few more rapidly delivered sentences—"good-bye."

Vance had never received a thank-you statement quite like that. Each year for the next thirty to thirty-five years, Vance received a telephone call from the rabbi on New Year's Day, always brisk, clever, short. Vance imagined the small rabbi, in full clothing, sitting in his study, calling hundreds of people he felt attached to by some happening—tragedy or otherwise. One year, there was no call on New Year's Day. A few days later, the son of the rabbi called, he had trouble calling everyone that his father called, there were so many on the list. His father had died. He too was a rabbi. Later when Vance moved, he received no more calls, but the rabbi's son called Vance's son on New Year's Day when he could not find Vance's new phone number.

Vance thought often of the rabbi. In addition to the phone calls, Vance noted an increase in the number of his private practice patients from New York. When Vance was ill with cancer of the colon, his own minister came for a visit—Daddy King came, and yes, a rabbi from New York came. The rabbi traveled on to the Western Wall where he placed a note asking for a good surgical result.

The rabbi was an unforgettable person, who talked rapidly, was always brief, but was soaking wet with compassion and kindness.

29

Infrastructure

Dr. Vance Connelly was an early riser. He discovered long ago that his brain worked better in the early morning. He could solve a vexing problem early in the morning that he could not solve the night before. In medical school, he studied at night but reviewed the information in the morning at 4:00 AM. Later, he established his two-chair concept. He sat in one chair to work and study. When he could not solve a medical or emotional problem, he sat in another chair in another room in order to think. This too was done at 4:00 AM.

Vance never believed he had more than an average brain; so recognizing that most people don't use all of their brains, he simply decided to use as much of his brain as he could. This worked well for him throughout his career.

As Vance climbed the academic ladder, he became aware of an important fact. He became aware of all the people that helped create the environment he worked in. The colleagues, the medical students, house officers and fellows, the nurses, the physician assistants, the ward clerks, and administrators. He understood that there would be no Vance without them. He arrived at the hospital at 6:00 AM and saw the night crew, which consisted of the men and women who swept the floors and cleaned the toilets. He knew them all and told them frequently, "You do a great job, and we could not do our work without you."

One of the ladies who swept the floors was from Vietnam. She had several children. Two of her children were physicians, one was a computer expert, and one was a tailor. She always greeted Vance as he walked down the hall. She would occasionally give him very large oranges.

The lady who cleaned the toilets was quiet but competent; when Vance thanked her for her work, she smiled and nodded her head.

Vance made a mental note of this and hoped that when everyone talked about *infrastructure*, they remembered that infrastructure included people, many of whom are dedicated to the creation of excellence.

30

Apoptosis and Red Roses

Dr. Vance Connelly moved into Brookland when he was eighty-four years old, six months after his wife died of cancer of the pancreas. Connelly continued to teach medicine at Greystone University until he was eighty-eight years of age.

The people at Brookland retirement facility (community as they liked to call it) had many health problems, including heart and vascular disease and cancer. Some had obvious memory loss, especially those who entered there at age eighty and lived until they were ninety to one hundred years of age.

Vance, who had always believed that excellent medicine was the study of people, recognized the various medical conditions. A few residents developed acute health problems and became a red rose. To explain, when a resident died, a single red rose was placed in a vase located on a table where all could see the passing of a friend. The resident's name was shown as was the date of death. A book was placed nearby, stating when and where the service would be held. There also was a place where friends could sign up for the bus ride to the church where the service would be held. At times, only a few people signed the book. The person had outlived almost all of his or her friends.

Commonly, however, residents who entered the facility when they were seventy to eighty years of age were mobile, slow, yes, but needed no assistance. They also conversed well with others. Gradually, a few residents would notice that they dropped food on their napkins more than previously and developed a bit of unsteadiness when they made a sharp turn. They began to use a cane and touched the wall as they walked. After several months, they found that they needed a walker; the broader base helped steady them. As time passed, they began to use a wheelchair and hired the services of a sitter to push them around and help them in their apartment. They noticed a gradual weight loss and had more difficulty with eating and conversing. They gradually became extremely fragile. Some of them spent a week or so in the extended care area of the facility. Later they moved there permanently, and sold their apartment. Some of them died during sleep. There were no acute symptoms; they just slipped away. This,

Vance believed, was clustered apoptosis. You see, the cells that make up the body are programmed from their beginning to die, to wear out after a predetermined time. A pathologist can determine the difference in apoptosis, as this type of cell death is called, and the death of cells due to some acute disease. When the cells of many organs develop apoptosis, it leads to a quiet departure of the person from the world of the living.

Vance, as a physician, began to recognize the stages that preceded fragility and then noted the length of time the person lived in assisted care before they just slipped away.

We will all be red roses someday. Some of us will have acute conditions, and some of us will just fade away.

31

The Learning Center

Dr. Vance Connelly always reacted unfavorably when he encountered a building that was named the *Learning Center*. Toward the end of his thirty-year tenure as professor and chairman of the department of medicine at Greystone University, he noted that someone had named the room that housed a number of computers in the hospital as the *Learning Center*. This was frustrating to him, because he thought it should be named the *Information Center*.

One day, Vance noticed a temporary sign stating that "the *Learning Center* would be moving soon." Vance looked up and down the hall and saw no one; it was 6:00 AM. He thought that he must not be seen doing what he was about to do. Seeing no one, he took out his black magic marker and wrote on the sign, "The *Learning Center* is the brain. Where do you plan to move it?"

To this day, those in charge of the *Learning Center* do not know who wrote that message on the sign. (Dear reader, please don't tell anyone that a supposed to be dignified professor did it.)

32

A Day to Remember, or Forget[*]

Most of Vance Connelly's days went smoothly, as if every action and thought were well-oiled. There were days, however, that made up for them because every single event went wrong, like rust clogging up a water pipe.

Vance rose at 4:00 AM; he could not break the habit. He turned to switch on the light, and it gave a lightning flash; the bulb had blown out. He struggled to sit up, then he stood up. Where was his walking stick? He could not see in the dark. Oh, there it is. He touched it and heard it fall. He stooped in the dark to find it and tilted forward, almost falling.

---

[*] All of these things discussed in this essay did not happen the same day, but they all happened.

He recovered and switched the light on in the adjacent bathroom. Vance planned to take his usual morning shower. He routinely covered his hair with shampoo before stepping into the shower. He did so and turned on the water. It was ice-cold. He desperately turned the faucet, but it was cold. He went to the other bathroom, one used for visitors. Thank God there was hot water. He showered there, put on his white terry cloth robe, and, using his walking stick, struggled into the kitchen.

He needed a cup of coffee. He routinely used decaffeinated beans to make his coffee. He used a bean smasher so as not to burn the beans. He stored a small amount of ground coffee in an airtight container. He fancied himself as a little bit of an expert in the coffee-making process. He used Martinez coffee (his favorite) from Costa Rica.

This morning, he found his airtight container of coffee was empty; so at 4:15 AM, he had to smash some coffee beans while fearing he would wake up his neighbor in the apartment next door. But he had to have coffee.

He wanted a warm muffin to complete his breakfast. He placed it in the microwave and set the timer for twelve seconds, or he thought he set it for twelve seconds (turned out to be twelve minutes). He burned the muffin, which happened to be his last muffin.

To calm his nerves, he sat down in his large easy chair and placed his cup of coffee on a table to his right. He turned on his television, and white wiggly snow filled the screen—cable down!

The morning paper was usually delivered at 5:00 AM. Vance looked for his walking stick, which had fallen behind his chair. He almost fell trying to reach it. He then walked to the front door of his apartment, looked in the receptacle on the wall outside the entrance door—no newspaper.

Vance decided to get dressed. He could not find the blue shirt he wanted to wear. Oh, he remembered, it was at the laundry. He dressed slowly. Where was the shoehorn? He needed his shoehorn. He finally used a plastic bookmarker in place of a shoehorn.

Vance worked on a manuscript and then noted that the clock said 5:15 AM. He rushed to the elevator. He must not be late to the hospital. The elevator seemed not to work initially, but finally did. He noted in the lobby that there were two clocks; both said it was 6:00 AM. Vance was distressed; his watch was wrong. *Oh my god*, he thought, *I must not be late.* He moved as fast as he could to his car, which the valet placed near the entrance of the building. Vance saw it immediately, he had a flat tire. That did it. Vance knew he had lost the entire day to some unseen demon.

Vance somehow relaxed since his travel was out of the question. He called the hospital; one of the few times in his fifty-eight years at Greystone he did not keep his scheduled appointments.

Vance sat calmly in the lobby and waited for the AAA truck. He thought, *What was it Solomon said? Oh yes, he said, "This too shall pass."*

The moral of the story is just that. Whatever the thorns are that can ruin a day, it is true, *"This too shall pass."*

33

A Very Sad Day

The year was 1947, World War II was over. Dr. Vance Connelly was a captain in the United States Army. He, Jennifer, and little John lived in a suburb of Denver, Aurora. He was stationed at Fitzsimmons General Hospital. At the time of this event, he was serving as an internist on a general medicine floor of the main hospital. He was also assigned the duty of teaching those doctors who had been overseas for several years. Most of them outranked Connelly but appreciated his efforts.

Vance returned to his home in Aurora at about 6:00 PM. Jennifer was in the kitchen preparing dinner, which was always wonderful. She kissed Vance and said, "We had a call from home, but they would not talk to me. The person wanted to talk to you, she left her number." Vance thought this was strange because the call came from Jennifer's hometown, not his. He sat in the easy chair (at least it was the best chair they had near the telephone), dialed the number, wondering what was going on.

The lady on the phone said in an unsteady voice, "I am sorry . . . I regret . . . to tell you I have some very bad news [pause]. There has been a wreck; a drunken truck driver hit the car [pause]. Jennifer's mother was killed instantly [pause]. Jennifer's sister was driving . . . she is alive in the hospital, head damage and numerous bones broken, on critical list . . . her young son was killed, and another son injured. I am so sorry."

Vance was stunned; words did not come for a long time. He gained control of himself and said, "I will tell Jennifer. I am crushed and know she will be more than crushed, but she is strong. I will do my best for her (pause). Thank you for doing what you had to do. We will come as soon as possible."

Vance sat in the chair trying to muster the strength to tell Jennifer. He then walked into the kitchen to tell Jennifer the bad news. He loved her so very much, how could he tell her without hurting her?

Vance placed his arms around Jennifer and held her tight and said as softly as he could, "I have very bad news for you." As he told her, he hugged her tighter. She gasped, sobbed, slumped, but regained her strength and chose to sit in a chair as the tears came. After a few minutes, she said, "We must go home tomorrow."

Vance proceeded to obtain three airline tickets. The next morning, he obtained emergency leave, and they flew to Atlanta. The trip was uneventful, except young John became cyanotic and had to be relieved with oxygen.

Vance's mother and father met the three of them at the Atlanta airport. Vance and Jennifer traveled to see her unconscious sister in the hospital in Covington. Little John was cared for by Vance's parents.

Jennifer's sister had a severe head injury and numerous broken bones. She had lost considerable blood. Vance insisted that she be transfused and moved to Crawford Long Hospital in Atlanta where her orthopedic surgeon and neurologist could see her daily. This was accomplished, and Vance slept on a cot in her room for several weeks until she was able to go home.

Vance's leave time from the army was running out. He extended his leave but was then told that he could be released for hardship because the army was now decreasing its manpower since the war was over. Accordingly, Vance was honorably discharged a few months before his two-year tour of duty was completed.

Vance, Jennifer, and little John moved into the home of Jennifer's sister and helped with her rehabilitation. She did recover, but was seriously limited because of the many broken bones and head injury.

In late 1947, when Jennifer's sister could function, Vance and Jennifer moved to Boston where Vance began his cardiology training at the Massachusetts General Hospital.

This sad story had a great influence on Vance and Jennifer's lives, because, some years later, after Vance was well established at Greystone University Hospital, he was called to serve out his unfinished tour of duty in the navy. He was assigned to the National Navy Medical Center in Bethesda, Maryland, a suburb of Washington, D.C. (But that is another story.)

34

Ears Are Not Very Pretty but—

This essay about the ears is possible, because Vance Connelly began to lose his hearing at the age of sixty-five. He followed in the footsteps of his father who also became deaf in his sixties.

As one of the six senses, the ear permits a person to hear and keep his or her balance. Vance was intrigued to learn that people laughed at and made jokes about the utterances made by those who were deaf.

Jennifer, Vance's wife, was the first to notice that his hearing was diminishing. Vance denied it because he could still hear heart sounds and murmurs that younger trainees could not hear. He did not perceive that this was the normal sequence of events, like the old football player that could still outdo the rookies because the skill of playing football involves many talents other than strength. Vance finally accepted the fact when, in a teaching conference, a smart young woman presented her findings on a patient, and Vance could not hear a single word she uttered. The pitch of her voice matched Vance's hearing defect. Vance decided to surprise Jennifer by going to the audiologist to get fitted for hearing aids. At that point in time, his hearing loss enabled him to wear the in-the-canal hearing aids that were not visible. He then invited Jennifer to go out for dinner. Vance was disappointed when Jennifer did not instantly notice the difference in his hearing, so he finally told her about his new hearing aids. She was very happy, and they then had a great dinner.

Over the next several years, Vance was forced to get the stronger behind-the-ear hearing aids. He initially resisted this progression, but it was needed because the in-the-canal aids were not adequate. With the passage of time, Vance stopped worrying about whether or not anyone could see his hearing aids.

People laugh at, or with, deaf people because deaf people often give inappropriate responses to other people's questions or statements. Vance was eventually able to join in the laughter when he perceived he had made an inappropriate response, but it also forced him to say less than he formerly did and led him to phrase his comments so that the other person could answer using only a few words. He learned, however, that some people can't talk using only a few words; they talk in paragraphs, making it impossible for the deaf person to determine the subject of the sentences they are muttering.

Vance was very surprised to discover that very few people know anything about hearing (that included doctors) unless they were specifically trained to be eye, ear, nose, and throat (EENT) doctors. The young trainee may write in the workup of a patient that the EENT is normal, but when asked, "Did you check the patient's hearing or vision?" the answer is usually no. Dr. Vance Connelly was then known to say, "The ears are not very pretty, but they enable us to hear and keep our balance. You forgot to check those items in your patient. You must never write or say that something is normal when you have not checked it. It is OK to state 'not examined,' but it is not OK to say something is normal when you have not examined it."

Peculiar things happen that prove the lack of understanding people in general have about deafness.

For example, suppose the deaf person finds himself sitting at a dining table for four. Let us assume they all can see the person's behind-the-ear hearing aids. Initially the other three diners make an effort to talk to the person who is deaf. So far, so good. Within a minute or two, the other three diners begin to talk to each other. The deaf person can't distinguish what they are saying and tunes them out. Thirty minutes pass, and one of the other diners will say, "You are not talking much. What's up?" As a result, deaf persons prefer to eat at a table for two, the other person has no one else to talk to but the one who is deaf.

Most people don't understand that a deaf person with hearing aids hears a great deal. The aids are supposed to augment certain frequencies of sound that can no longer be heard. Up to a point, they can do that; but as time passes, they can't replace a severe loss of frequencies. Talking louder will not help. The deaf person with aids can hear a great deal, noises, metallic clashes, etc. This leads to a serious and painful error; a person seeing the hearing aid thinks, *Aha, the person is deaf. I will place my lips near his ear and yell.* This, of course, almost kills the deaf person, and he moves his head away from the yelling person. The yelling person may deduce that he has not yelled loud enough and follows the deaf person's head yelling even louder than before. The voice explodes like a bomb in the deaf person's ear.

Please, the way to talk to a deaf person with hearing aids is to face the deaf person; keep your hands from covering your lips. Most deaf people can read lips; some can do this very well. Speak normally and distinctly. Do not rattle off long sentences. The deaf person is trying to find the subject of your sentences and hopes to make a response that fits your question or statement. Loud conversations around the deaf person with aids prevent hearing. The deaf person may hear well in a quiet room.

One reason a deaf person with aids has trouble hearing on the phone is that he or she cannot see the lips of the person on the other end of the line.

Hearing aids have improved greatly, but much advertising is just that—a company pays an advertiser to create a beautiful brochure extolling why their hearing aids are the best. Unfortunately, advances in technology come slowly.

Finally, we should all pity those who are destroying their ears with loud music. We should do something about this, but like smoking, it is an addiction.

Although it is advertised on television, few people have ever heard of the special telephone service that converts a person's talking to written captions. It is provided without charge by the telephone company.

Vance gets by with his deafness but longs to once again hear the high pitch of a leaking aortic valve, the wind, the drops of rain, the song of a bird, beautiful music, and the sound of Jennifer's voice.

35

Slippery Ankles

The old University Hospital in Augusta, Georgia, was a great place to train. Interns and residents in medicine were in awe of Dr. Sydenstricker. He was the smartest doctor Vance Connelly ever knew. Unlike today, where there are many smart people in specialized areas of medicine, Dr. Sydenstricker was an expert in neurology, dermatology, nutrition, gastroenterology, hematology, and you name it. Vance was lucky to have the chance to work with him as an intern and resident. There were few house officers because in 1944 and 1945, World War II was still raging. There was no on-and-off schedule. You admitted patients and you dismissed them—that was the schedule. The lack of sleep was never discussed.

The medical wards of the hospital were divided into Barret 1-2 and Lamar. They were large, open wards with beds for many patients. They were segregated—Barret

1-2 was for white patients, and Lamar was for black patients. White nurses were called Miss So-and-So, and black nurses were called Nurse So-and-So. Penicillin was just becoming available.

Dr. Sydenstricker was famous for asking the right questions. He asked one patient, "Do you raise beans?"

"Yes, I do," responded the patient. Aside, Dr. Sydenstricker said, "Check him for arsenic poisoning." He knew that some farmers in the area sprayed their beans with an arsenic solution to prevent unwanted bugs.

Vance saw his only case of pellagra during his residency. The patient had dermatitis, diarrhea, and esophageal damage that prevented the treatment with oral nicotinic acid, so an associate of Dr. Sydenstricker's prepared an intravenous preparation of nicotinic acid. Vance was asked to administer it. He did. The patient tolerated it and recovered. As far as Vance knows, he gave the first intravenous nicotinic acid that was ever given.

Amid the night-and-day work, some unusual things happened. One day, Vance walked on the Lamar Ward. A middle-aged woman was standing in a large open window, her head bent, her two hands clasped in front of her like she was about to dive, her hospital gown flowing in front of her leaving her backside "undressed." She said nothing, but it was obvious—she planned to dive out the window. Vance rushed to her side and grabbed her ankles. About that time, Curley arrived. Curley was the brilliant, ever-present, bald-headed resident in OB-GYN. Curley grabbed one of the jumping patient's ankles, and Vance held the other one. It was fortunate that this was all taking place on the second floor of the hospital because the house officer quarters were on the first, or ground, floor. They yelled and yelled to attract the attention of the other interns and residents below. They yelled, "Get a blanket! Get a blanket! Catch this woman." Curley and Vance tried their best to hold on to her, but as she threw her body out the window, they felt her legs slipping from their grip. They were able to hold her long enough for four interns and residents to place a blanket perfectly beneath her, with each one holding up a corner. As she fell, she turned over once and landed with great precision in the middle of the blanket. She was then transferred to the psychiatric service.

And so it went, World War II raged, Roosevelt died, the atom bomb was dropped, and hospitals were built so that it was difficult for a disturbed patient to jump from their hospital room.

36

Golf

Dr. Vance Connelly, his wife Jennifer, and their three young sons were traveling home from church in their new Buick on Powers Ferry Road. Vance was driving about thirty miles per hour. It was a beautiful spring day—green trees, beautiful grass, wonderful smells. Powers Ferry Road was adjacent to an excellent public golf course.

Just as the world seemed to be saying how lucky you five people are, a golf ball hit the windshield. The nonbreakable glass shattered; white lines spread over most of the left side of the windshield.

Vance was shocked as were all of the members of his family. He stopped the car, lowered his window, and saw a very upset man with a golf club swaggering up to the car. Vance just sat there bewildered, wondering what was about to happen.

The man came within a few inches of the car, near Vance's nose, and said while gritting his teeth, "Look what you have done. Damn, you have ruined my Sunday." He left shaking his golf club at Vance.

Vance decided not to argue with him and drove quietly home.

37

Sunshine

His name was Sunshine, it really was, Harry Sunshine. He was about five feet ten inches tall, pattern baldness, sort of a Roman nose, tan complexion, about sixty-five years old. He was a merchant.

He was one of Dr. Vance Connelly's patients and knew that Vance treated children as well as adults with heart disease. He also knew that Vance was worried about one of his patients, a child with rheumatic heart disease.

Mr. Sunshine showed up at Vance's office, which was at Greystone University Hospital, with a load of something. He asked to see Vance.

Vance, who always enjoyed seeing Harry, said, "Hello. What have you there?"

"I have some things for you," Harry replied. With that, he opened the bags. Vance was amazed; all the bags were filled with toys.

Vance said, "Oh, Harry, how nice of you to bring all those toys for my little patients. Come, let's go to the hospital room where my sickest patient is so you can give her one of the toys."

"No, no, Doc, you don't understand. I give you the toy, and you give it to her, maybe that will help her get well, the more she likes and trusts you, the more likely she is to get well."

Vance did as he was told because it was obvious; Harry knew that kindness and trust were essential elements of good doctoring.

Later Vance discovered that Harry Sunshine was the kindest man in town who got his emotional kicks from acts such as he had witnessed.

Vance often wondered about the origin of the Sunshine name; but, however it happened and whoever was responsible got it right, this Sunshine brought sunshine!

38

Maturity

This story is about Vance Connelly's youngest son, Phil. The following event occurred when Phil was about ten years old.

"Dad," he said, "I hate girls." He probably uttered that he wanted to be a fireman when he grew up, or a cowboy or a race car driver. He was sure about one thing, he did not like girls.

About two weeks later, Vance returned home from Greystone University Hospital to find Phil sitting in Vance's large brown lounge chair. He had the telephone to his ear. Vance paused, out of sight, to capture the scene and determine what was going on. Vance waited, and waited. Phil was obviously talking to a girl. Phil finally finished.

"I thought you didn't like girls. Just a few days ago, you told me that you did not like girls."

Phil was quick to answer as he marched out of the room with his head high and two arms swinging, "Last week, Dad, I was very immature!"

Vance smiled and thought, *I no longer have a really young son.*

39

Thank You Again and Again

Dr. Vance Connelly will not forget Mrs. Sonova. She was about eighty years old, a little plump, smart, with dark brown hair and designer glasses. She was sick with atherosclerosis involving the coronary arteries along with hypertension. When Vance initially saw her, her memory was intact.

Christmas was coming soon. Vance was surprised and pleased with the large ham and Swiss cheese package sent to him by Mrs. Sonova. He went directly to the phone and told her how much he appreciated the gift. In a few days, another ham and Swiss cheese package arrived at Vance's home. Vance was pleased but concerned. He wondered why Mrs. Sonova had sent another gift that was identical to the first one. He went to the phone and called Mrs. Sonova. "Mrs. Sonova," Vance said, "you must have misunderstood my previous call where I thanked you for the lovely gift. I just received another package that is similar to the first one. I do thank you, but that is just too generous." In a few days, another package arrived at Vance's home. Yes, it contained a large ham with Swiss cheese.

Vance did not call again, for it was obvious Mrs. Sonova had lost her short-term memory. Mrs. Sonova's mind was centered on sending a ham and Swiss cheese package to Vance, but she did not remember actually sending it, so she sent the gift to Vance on three different occasions.

40

Fried Chicken and Altruism

Vance's wife, Jennifer, lived for her three children. She could be gentle or firm, depending on the problem at hand. The kids knew she would sacrifice her own comfort, emotionally and physically, for them. They loved her deeply. She was a great mother and was the major influence on the rearing of their three sons to manhood. At the table, she knew what the kids liked. She would usually give them a larger portion of a dish they liked and at times would give them a part of her share.

There was one exception to this motherly altruism. The secret was learned years later by their middle son, Steve, who laughed when he told others about it. "Mom," he said, "always would give us more than our own share of favorite food. But I did not know until I was in college that the breast was the choice piece of a chicken. When we had chicken, Mom always insisted that she eat the breast and Dad eat the wing, which was his favorite piece. I thought, because of her routine unselfishness, that the breast must be the worst piece of chicken, because she always, I mean always, ate it."

41

Mississippi Remembered

This story could have happened anywhere, but it happened in Mississippi. Mississippi, the land of beautiful trees, Southern homes, and classic literature.

Dr. Vance Connelly had been asked to visit the medical school in Jackson. Dr. Harper Hellems, the chief of medicine there, was Connelly's host. The purpose of the visit was for Connelly to give several teaching sessions to the medical students, interns, and residents at the medical school. This was, and still is, a common practice that attempts to show the trainees what is happening elsewhere. The only difference is that forty years ago, the visiting professors saw, diagnosed, and recommended treatment of patients he or she saw with trainees. Now, the visiting professor usually does not see patients, does not speak to trainees, gives one or two lectures on the results of clinical trials or basic science, and leaves. Connelly always saw patients and spent most of his time with trainees.

Dr. Hellems was the excellent chief of medicine at the medical school that was famous for its physiology department and cardiac transplant efforts.

The plane trip to Jackson was uneventful and quick. Dr. Hellems was waiting at the gate when the plane landed. He joined Vance to get his suitcase, and they walked a short distance to Dr. Hellems's car.

There it was, a beautiful sports car. Beautiful, but a bit small. When Vance slipped into the front passenger seat, he felt it happen. Nothing like that had ever happened to Vance, and nothing like that has happened to him since that fateful day. The happening was an oxymoron, serious but funny. As he slipped into his seat, Vance felt the bottom of his pants being torn. He slid back and stood up to inspect the damage. There was a tear, several inches long, that created a flap that dropped down and exposed his underwear.

What to do became a very important subject. Vance's first teaching session was scheduled to begin in about thirty minutes. The medical school was several miles from the airport. There was insufficient time to go to a men's store and buy a new pair of pants. They rushed to Dr. Hellems's office with Vance holding up the flap of pants with his hand. Dr. Hellems explained the emergency to his secretary. She asked Vance to step into the next room and pull off his pants. He did so and handed the pants to her through a crack in the doorway. She handed Vance a pair of surgical blues, and Vance put them on. She was going to mend the flap in his pants and, for some reason, had the equipment to do so. So there Vance stood in his coat, his tie, and the hospital's surgical blue pants. The clock was ticking. Vance's first teaching session, medical grand rounds, was to begin in less than ten minutes.

Forty years have passed, and Vance cannot remember whether he conducted grand rounds wearing his surgical blues or if the secretary was successful in her efforts to mend the flap in the bottom of his pants in time for him to wear them at the teaching session.

Vance saw and diagnosed the patient in front of an audience of forty or more medical students and house officers. The lower part of the patient's face was thin due to atrophy of the masseter muscles, and his neck was small due to atrophy of the neck muscles. Vance shook the patient's hand. The patient continued to hold Vance's hand because his hand muscles would not relax, a definite clue to the diagnosis. Vance said, "I believe the patient has myotonic dystrophy, a genetically determined condition, and auscultation of the heart, and the electrocardiogram may reveal a conduction abnormality in the heart."

Vance left Mississippi with his flap mended, thanks to a talented secretary. Although Vance made numerous teaching trips, he has never forgotten that one and was also pleased that, under the stress of the flap, he was still able to function and correctly diagnose the patient.

42

Cigarettes

I have never smoked. Somehow, I withstood the peer pressure of youth and never touched the deadly things.

Fast-forward to 1971. I was in Charlottesville, Virginia, attending former president Lyndon Johnson who had experienced his second heart attack and had been admitted to the university hospital. I had been LBJ's cardiologist since July 1955 when the president had his first heart attack. Now out of office, he had no one to meet the press, so he asked me to meet with a large number of reporters and photographers who had gathered at the hospital.

The press conference went well, and I was pleased with the outcome, but not for long.

A few days later, I received a phone call from my friend, former surgeon general Luther Terry. Our friendship started several years earlier when both of us were in Washington. Luther had borrowed one of my uniforms to wear in the play *The Cain Mutiny*. Luther was an amateur actor, but this time, on the phone, he was not acting. He said in a firm voice, "Willis, how could you? Why did you do that?"

"Do what, Luther?"

"Smoke right in front of the cameras of all those photographers."

"Luther, I don't smoke—I never have. I have urged everyone I know to stop smoking, including the president, and he did."

Luther responded, "Willis, I saw you."

My mental wheels were turning. I figured out what must have happened. I always carried three-by-five-inch index cards with me. I used them to write notes on when the need arose. I remembered, nervous as I was meeting with the press, I had rolled one of the cards up and held it in my fingers; it must have looked like a cigarette. I explained the event to Luther who was much relieved, for he was the surgeon general who first forced the cigarette industry to stamp each pack of cigarettes with the statement *Smoking Cigarettes Is Dangerous to Your Health.*

A few days later, I received a hostile phone call from the president of the heart association who was in Hawaii. He was irate.

He said, "Why did you do that?"

I knew what "that" was and explained the event to him. I explained again and again and again.

One would think that the explanation of the event to these two individuals would end the story, but I was, at that time, president of the American Heart Association (AHA). The AHA had taken its stand against smoking tobacco, undoubtedly influenced by Dr. Paul White, who had played a major role in the creation of the AHA. I had trained with Dr. White at the Massachusetts General Hospital in Boston, and he was one of my mentors. So to my chagrin, there was a bit of rumbling within the top officials of the AHA about what had happened.

To counter the rumbling, I presented a detailed explanation of the event to an official gathering of the leadership of the AHA.

In brief, I never smoked; but for a while, I had a hard time convincing everyone that I did not.

PS: This is the second story in which my real name is used rather than my pen name. My friend and patient LBJ would want everyone to use real names in a story that involved him.

43

A Call at 11:00 PM

Dr. Vance Connelly reached for the ringing telephone. It was eleven o'clock at night. The bed felt good after a long day.

After a brief hello by Vance, the lady said, "Dr. Connelly, I remember you told me that it would be wise not to get pregnant. Well, it just happened."

Vance remembered the patient even though he had been away, on duty at the National Naval Medical Center in Bethesda. He remembered her; she had severe rheumatic heart disease. This was in 1956, before surgeons were removing and replacing the aortic valve.

Vance said (and gave her name, but it will not be revealed here), "Since it just happened, maybe you are not pregnant."

"Oh," she said.

"Wait a few weeks."

"OK."

It turned out she was not pregnant. That is the last time Vance heard from her.

The moral of this short story is that some patients do listen to their doctor.

44

Mumps and Dancing

It was 1957, and Dr. Vance Connelly had recently been appointed professor and chairman of the department of medicine of Greystone University. He was selected when he was thirty-five years old and began his work when he was thirty-six.

Jennifer Connelly, Vance's wife, was pleased that Vance had finally agreed to take dancing lessons. Vance had, for a number of years, been able to avoid such an encounter. She liked to dance, and so did he, but dancing lessons were not his cup of tea. He might be seen at the studio, and he had always felt a little strange when he saw a couple dancing some new step—revealing the hours they had spent trying to look like Fred and Ginger. He usually made every excuse in the book in an effort to escape. Finally, however, he agreed; he would take dancing lessons with her.

Vance's youngest son had the common childhood disease—mumps—first. That is, he was the first in the Connelly family to have the mumps. The middle son was the next to have mumps. He had a tough time—mumps encephalitis. The oldest son was next, completing the spread of mumps in the Connelly family, or so Vance thought.

The night before the scheduled dance lesson, Vance told Jennifer, "I think I am coming down with the mumps." Jennifer responded rather quickly, "Don't come up with another excuse, we are going to modernize our dancing."

"I know, I know we are going to do that, but please don't tell anyone. This proves, without a doubt, how much I love you."

Silence for a few minutes.

Once again, Vance said very quietly, "I am almost certain I am coming down with the mumps!"

With that, Jennifer felt both sides of Vance's face and said, "I don't see or feel anything. You are kidding me."

"No, I kid you not."

"OK, we will see. But I tell you, tomorrow one side of your face had better be swollen."

The next day, the answer was obvious, Vance's face was warped out of shape; Vance had mumps. He smiled;

she frowned and was not too happy calling to break their dancing lesson appointment.

The final touch to this short story appeared in the Atlanta newspaper. The exact words are not remembered, but the short paragraph went something like this:

> Greystone's newly appointed professor and chairman of the department of medicine is considered to be young—age thirty-six. He is now convalescing at his home from the childhood disease, mumps.

Jennifer got a kick out of that—and bless her—she never made another appointment for the two of them to modernize their dancing.

45

A Night in Jail

Jennifer never wanted her husband, Dr. Vance Connelly, to tell this story. She was afraid the gossip chatter would get it wrong. Vance told it a few times, but Jennifer won the debate, and Vance seldom mentioned his night in jail.

It happened one night in 1942; Vance and Jennifer were not married. Vance was beginning his second year in medical school at the University of Georgia School of Medicine in Augusta, Georgia, and Jennifer was teaching school in her small hometown, Jersey, Georgia. Vance, who was visiting Jennifer, was driving to Covington, Georgia, at about ten thirty at night to spend the night in a hotel when it happened.

Vance was traveling about thirty miles per hour on the right side of the curved road. Just as he hit the top of a small hill, another car was coming toward him on the wrong side of the road. The collision forced Vance's car into a rather large ditch. The other car pulled back, and the driver gunned the car over the hill, leaving Vance and his car stalled in the ditch. Vance never saw the driver's face.

Luck failed Vance; he could not get the car out of the ditch. Luck was with him in that he could open the car door on the driver's side and escape up to the road. Having reached the road, what now?

There were few houses in the area, and the houses that were barely seen had no lights. Although Vance had trouble seeing the road, he walked until he saw a lightless house near the road. Vance had to do it—he had to knock on the door and ask for help. The sleepy man came to the door and listened to Vance's story. Vance said, "May I use your phone so I can call the sheriff in Covington?"

Thank God he had a phone, and thank God he said, "Yup."

Vance called the sheriff and told his story. The sheriff said, "Stay where you are, I will come and get you."

The sheriff arrived some thirty minutes later. Vance was not sure that the sheriff believed he was a medical student, that the accident was not Vance's fault, and that Vance was not under the influence. He looked Vance over and over, asked him a few questions about the accident, but his questions gradually shifted to medical school and who Vance was visiting. He soon said, "Come on, son, I know the people in this area. I want us to make a visit on one of them."

Vance thanked the man who let him use the phone and sat beside the sheriff as he drove his car to another house about a mile away. They saw a car in the driveway, and the sheriff said, "There is a young man here—he drinks a bit too much and gives us trouble from time to time."

The sheriff knocked on the door and, when it was opened, said, "Is Darrell here?"

The man who opened the door said, "Yes, he is sound asleep."

"May I please see him?"

"Yes. I am telling you the truth."

The man led the sheriff and Vance into the young man's bedroom. The sheriff said, "Darrell, did you drive a car into the ditch?"

Darrell was rubbing his eyes with his hand and said, "No, I have been asleep for hours."

The sheriff said, "Darrell, the car is outside and you reek with the smell of alcohol. I don't believe you."

With that, the sheriff nodded to Vance and said, "Let's go. I will deal with Darrell later—when he is sober."

In the sheriff's car, the following rather remarkable conversation took place:

"So you gonna be a doctor?" the sheriff asked.

"Yes, sir," Vance said as he studied the sheriff's features for the first time. The sheriff had gray hair, a rather pink complexion, a small white mustache, a few wrinkles (more on his forehead than around his mouth), and a little extra fat around his waist. He appeared to be about sixty years of age. He carried a handgun.

The sheriff asked, "Where do you plan to spend the night?"

"I hope to spend it in the hotel in Covington. Then tomorrow, which is Sunday, I must try to get my car out of the ditch. I am sure it will need some repairs."

The sheriff said, "Tell you what—I'll take care of the car. I'll get it to the garage, but why don't you spend the night with me? My wife and I have plenty of room and would enjoy your visit."

The sheriff and his wife lived upstairs in the county jail. The decor was late nineteenth century—the "house" was their castle. Vance's bed was very comfortable.

The next morning, the sheriff's white-haired wife invited Vance to breakfast. Vance will never forget it—eggs, ham, homemade biscuits, coffee, toast, jelly, all you could eat.

Vance had never been treated with more kindness. He called Jennifer and said, "You won't believe what I am about to tell you."

Jennifer's mother loaned Vance her car to use until his was repaired. The repair work took about two weeks.

So that is the story of how Vance spent a night in jail.

46

Jokes: Or Are They?

Dr. Vance Connelly remembers when he became chairman of the department of medicine at Greystone University. He had much advice, and fortunately, many excellent people wanted to help him, the youngster who was to lead them. This story is about two jokes that linger indelibly in his memory. These jokes may not be funny to everyone and did not involve Vance, but there are messages in them that could apply to any leader of any enterprise. Vance doesn't know who created them, but these jokes were very well known in the fifties.

Joke number 1. The new leader of the department arrived on the scene. He went to his future office, the one that would be his the next day. He encountered the leader who was leaving and said, "I am so glad I caught you here. Please, I need your help. Do you have any advice for me?"

"Pleased to see you. Congratulations. I am sure you will do fine. The previous leader helped me a lot. He explained the three envelopes in the desk drawer. In fact, I have left similar letters for you. What is written in them will help you a great deal. The envelopes are numbered 1, 2, and 3. You should open number 1 in a few months, then open number 2 a few months later, and open number 3 a few months after that. The wise advice written in the envelopes will help you greatly."

"Thank you. Thank you. Good luck to you in your new life."

The new leader went to work. Things did not go well. He tried but made no headway. He opened envelope number 1. The note said: *Emphasize that you are new to the job. Ask everyone to give you a little more time.*

A few more months passed. Complaints were increasing. The new leader felt he needed some new advice. He opened envelope number 2. The note said: *Blame everything that has gone wrong on your predecessor.*

For the next few months, the new leader did that. His predecessor left a mess, but he believed he was getting hold of it. He then sensed that he was in trouble, no one listened to him. He desperately needed to know what advice was written in envelope number 3. He opened enveloped number 3. There was the answer, terse and clear: *Resign as quickly as possible, create three envelopes, they, whoever they are, are about to fire your——.*

The other joke, if that is what it is, deals with climbing up and down the academic ladder.

Once upon a time, there was a very nice, talented, respected young man who worked in a very good circus. He worked hard and became a trapeze artist. In fact, he became the very best performer on the high trapeze. At the pinnacle of his career, he was heralded as the best in the business. Books were written about him, movies were made, every kid wanted to do what he did.

As time passed, he began going down the ladder of achievement. He was no longer at the top of his game, younger guys were outperforming him. But he continued to work because he loved the circus. He slipped more each year until he became the person who cleaned up the elephant bin. He did that without complaint because, to say once again, he really loved the circus atmosphere.

One day, a middle-aged man and his wife saw the former trapeze artist cleaning out the elephant bin. They recognized him and said, "We are so glad to see you. You are the greatest, no one can touch your ability. We saw you perform twenty-five years ago. But what are you doing here cleaning out the elephant bin?"

The former trapeze artist said, "Well, as time passed, I could not do what I used to do."

The middle-aged man said, "Well, why didn't you quit? You must have made enough money to retire."

The former trapeze artist said in a loud voice that reeked with the combination of surprise, determination, and sorrow, "*What*," with emphasis on the word, "*and give up show business?*"

General MacArthur said, "Old soldiers, never die; they just fade away." The same is true for old doctors and old teachers.

Jokes: or are they?

47

A Lesson Learned*

Vance was in the eighth grade; he sat with about twenty-four other students in the biology class. He liked the subject. He enjoyed discussing how the organs worked to make a living animal. He was especially interested in dissecting a frog.

The teacher was interested in the subject. He wore black horn-rimmed glasses, had straight black hair parted on the left, a rather red face just short of handsome, a Roman nose with larger than usual nostrils. He usually wore gray suits, talked clearly,

---

* The author has told and written this story many times. As told here, it is slightly different from the story that was told previously, because others were asked about that remarkable day. Accordingly, permission to reprint is not needed.

was calm. He entertained the students. He was a true teacher because he led the students to use their books to answer questions they generated on their own.

One day, just as the class was beginning, there was a loud knock on the door. The teacher went to the door, and the math teacher stormed into the room. The math teacher was also admired by the students, but they had never seen him so upset. He was physically trim, with splashes of gray hair above his ears. He had rimless glasses, a peaked nose, a heavy beard that he kept shaved, a red face that was redder than usual, and clinched fists. Today he was trembling with anger that was revealed in his shaky voice.

What came out of his mouth is only vaguely remembered. He snarled something like this: "You did it, I just found out."

The biology teacher said, "Calm down. What did I do?"

The math teacher inched closer to his opponent and held up his clinched fist, or was it both fists?

Vance was petrified as were the other students. The conversation and near fight continued between their favorite teachers, but no one remembers exactly what happened. The math teacher left the room, and the upset biology teacher slumped into his chair and placed his head between his hands and shook his head.

After the interruption, altercation, stunning performance, the biology teacher stood up, smiled, and reached for a stack of white paper. He then gave several sheets to the students who were sitting at the front desk of each row of seats. They were to give each of the students in their row a sheet of paper. The purpose of the theatrics became clear. The questions on the paper were "What were the first words uttered by the math teacher?" "What were the last words?" "What color tie did the math teacher have on?" The biology teacher knew that the students could not correctly answer the questions. He smiled and said, "Don't let your emotions stand in the way of your observations."

He made his point in an unforgettable way. He also said, "Today we begin the study of psychology, which I define as what makes people do what they do."

As Vance grew older, he understood how difficult it was to get the truth from questioning patients about their symptoms or previous illnesses. He understood also how witnesses to the same crime might give different answers to an investigator's questions. He also understood how the inaccurate tales of gossip grew.

This particular story must end with the disclaimer that what is written here may not be accurate. Vance talked to one of his former classmates who was in the room that memorable day, and she does not remember the story exactly as Vance recalled, once again proving that one's emotions can interfere with one's observations. She was certain it was their chemistry teacher who stormed into the room and not the math teacher. She did not recall what the argument was about, much less, what color his tie was.

48

From Here?

A young Vance Connelly, M.D., was seeing an eighty-five-year-old woman from the Panama Canal in his examining room. She was a little on the plump side and sat demurely in one of the chairs. Vance talked with her, tried to place her at ease, asked about her children and gradually gathered her complaints and symptoms. She relaxed and smiled throughout the interview.

Vance asked her, "Jump up on the examining table please. I want to examine your heart." Her chair was perhaps four feet from the table.

With that, her smile changed to a frown. Her face showed distress. Her voice was a mixture of fear and anxiety. Her voice trembled as she barely mumbled, "From here? I can't jump that far."

Vance realized his error and apologized, "Oh my, I did not mean that I wanted you to actually jump from your chair to the examining table. Forgive me. It was a poor choice of words." He then helped her to the examining table.

A young Vance Connelly was learning— communication is tricky, one must be careful and choose the correct words, else the message may be misinterpreted. He never used those words again.

49

An Intruder!

It happened in the middle of 2008. Vance Connelly had been at Brookland for four years. Vance had a longtime habit of taking a warm shower before he shaved. He understood that others shaved before they showered, but he stuck to his routine, which was to shower and then shave before he picked up his pen at 4:00 AM. He then wrote down whatever came to mind, sometimes scientific medical pieces and sometimes fiction. He did this until about 5:30 AM, when he went to Greystone University Hospital.

So on this particular morning, he stepped out of the shower. He always thought about the water. He thanked God for the warm water. Many people like cold water, but he really liked warm water. He often remembered that on one occasion, he had shampoo on his hair, stepped in the shower area, and there was only cold water. That is when he became even more convinced that a warm shower was God's gift to civilization.

Vance stepped out of the shower, dried off, and, in his birthday suit, began the ornery and usually routine task of shaving. Vance glanced down and lowered his arms and noticed a pair of black shoes in the doorway of the bathroom. He realized that the shoes were attached to two legs. As he raised his eyes, he noticed the legs were covered with a black dress. Strangely, he thought to himself that someone had broken into his apartment, but he was not alarmed or frightened. He wondered why he was not alarmed. There he was in this birthday suit, and someone was standing three feet away. *Maybe she has a gun,* he thought, but he was abnormally calm. He raised his eyes a little higher and recognized the face of the African American lady from Brookland security. He knew he was not in danger and frantically covered himself with a towel.

Vance knew her. In fact, he saw her every morning as he left Brookland on his way to Greystone. He asked, "What are you doing here?" He thought that was a reasonable question to ask at 4:00 AM.

She replied, "Your alarm signal went off. I assumed you needed help, so here I am."

Vance replied, "I did not signal anyone."

With that, the lady walked behind Vance and reached up and turned off the alarm switch. Vance must have accidentally turned it on when he closed the shower curtain.

50

A Twice-Told Story[*]

Vance told this story many times, but it was not always understood.

A pharmacist gave a lecture to the residents of Brookland, Atlanta's premier retirement home. The lecture dealt with the use of aspirin to prolong life.

Vance was unable to go to the lecture because of his work at Greystone University Hospital. He later asked one of the ladies, "What did the speaker say?"

The lady, who was in her early nineties, responded, "She said if we would take aspirin, we would live longer."

---

[*] This story was told first in J. W. Hurst, *The Last Leaf Has Fallen* (Xlibris Corporation, 2007). The author owns the copyright.

Vance said, "She may be right, but you do have to be careful because aspirin can cause stomach bleeding."

"Oh," she said, "I have been taking aspirin for years, but when she said it would make me live longer, I decided to stop taking it."

Many elderly people have already beaten the survival statistics and are no longer trying to live forever, or at least it is no longer a major goal in their lives. They want to do what they want to do and eat what they want to eat and be as happy as they can be.

51

And the Preacher Kept Preaching

The minister was preaching. Some members of the congregation were listening, or pretending to. Mr. Brown was not. He slept and snored until his wife poked her thumb in his back.

The minister was about half through his sermon when it happened. Mr. Boatwright gave a groan. He was sitting in the middle of another section of seats from where Vance and Jennifer were sitting. Vance rushed to his side. Those who sat next to Mr. Boatwright were preventing him from falling. In fact, as usually happens, people try to force a fainted person to sit, or stand, whereas nature knows best, the person should be allowed to fall gently so that their head is as low as the rest of their body. Vance did that, the preacher kept preaching, but the members of the congregation were looking at the commotion.

Vance had great difficulty kneeling on his artificial knees—his own knees were replaced a few months earlier. But the task at hand dominated the moment; he went down on his knees in order to examine Mr. Boatwright. He was surrounded by about five people helping all they could while Vance set about determining if Mr. Boatwright had simply fainted or if he had something more serious, such as cardiac arrest. So he quickly felt the carotid pulse, there was none. He placed his left ear to the chest, there was no heartbeat. Mr. Boatwright was not breathing. All of this signaled that Mr. Boatwright had cardiac arrest. He was well-known and loved by the members of the congregation; they knew he had some type of heart trouble. Vance shook his head, and the preacher kept preaching.

Vance made a fist of his right hand and pounded Mr. Boatwright in the middle of his chest. Those around him gasped; the preacher kept preaching.

Mr. Boatwright moved his legs, then his arms, then rolled his head. The people around him gasped again; the preacher kept preaching.

Mr. Boatwright began to talk, and the paramedics marched up the aisle, someone had called 911. The preacher kept preaching. The paramedics transported him to the hospital. Vance, still on his knees, could not get up. Two members of the congregation helped him to the upright position. Vance joined Jennifer as the closing hymn was sung.

The next Sunday at church, two elderly ladies approached Vance and said, "We were here last Sunday. We were thinking we would like to sit near you, would you mind?"

52

On Leadership

"What makes one a leader?" the little boy asked. "My teacher wants me to write about it."

The old, old man answered, "No one really knows."

"But what do you think?" the youngster asked. "How do you know who to vote for, for president?"

"I do know there are two extremes," the man with the white beard answered as he placed his arthritic hand on the child's head.

"What are they?"

"The one extreme leader follows the words of the famous French politician. I have forgotten his name." The old man closed his eyes and shook his head in an effort to remember.

"What did he say?"

He said something like this, "There goes my people, I must find out where they are going so I can go lead them!"

The child asked, "But he or she is not a leader in ideas, he only helps the people do what they want to do."

"That's true, but hear me out. The second type of leader, described in detail, is the smart, capable, studious leader who has many ideas. In fact, he or she has so many ideas that the population at large cannot mentally process them all. Unfortunately, he or she, this remarkable and unique leader, is so far ahead of the citizens that they cannot follow him or her, and they may not select him or her."

"Which type of leader do you prefer?"

The old man scratched his beard, threw up both hands, and said, "Neither one will be an ideal leader."

"What can we do? How do we know how to choose a leader?"

The old man, with a twinkle in his eyes, said, "You must learn to study the people who are running for office. You will undoubtedly want your choice to have some of the attributes that I discussed initially, that is, that he or she agrees with you on certain things. But you also want to give him or her a chance to implement some of his or her ideas. You want your leader to be a hybrid of the two extreme examples I discussed earlier."

"Won't that lead to confusion?"

The old man winked his eye and said, "You bet it will, I certainly hope it will."

"Why?"

"The final votes in an election will almost always be something like 52-48. Occasionally it may be 65-35. It will never be 100-0. This leads to arguments and confusion. The smart leader knows how to make a successful hybrid of leader 1 and leader 2. The trick is for the voter to accept that the right mix of leader 1 and 2 makes for successful progress. The loser must accept the winner, and the winner must accept the loser. The extent to which this is done determines the welfare and happiness of the people who the leader governs."

"My, my, that is complicated."

With that, the old man placed the palms of his two hands on the cheeks of the youngster and said, "Get used to it. We live in the greatest country of all, we are free to make a choice."

53

Accident?

Vance had been professor and chairman of the department of medicine at Greystone for five years and wanted to take a minisabbatical leave. He wanted to study for a few months with one of the world leaders in electrocardiography.

Vance secured a small grant from a private institution and took his whole family to Mexico City, obtained an apartment, and studied with a Communist Mexican. Vance, of course, did not know his teacher was a Communist before he left Greystone.

Initially, Vance's teacher tried to brainwash him about the virtues of Communism. Vance was impressed, not with Communism, but the brilliance of this teacher who knew more about Vance's congressmen and how they voted than he did. The indoctrination took place the day Vance reported in. Vance rejected the argument, so the subject was not raised again. To be on the safe side, Vance reported the event to the administrators at the American embassy. They said, "Don't worry. We have known about him for years. We watch him."

The traffic was so dangerous around Vance's apartment that he parked his Buick in the garage beneath the apartment building and walked to work each day. One day, a Sunday, Vance thought he would drive the Buick to take his family to see the wonderful sights of Mexico. He loaded the car with the family and eased it into the street that was filled with rapidly flowing traffic. That is when it happened.

Another car was in Vance's way. Although he was going about five miles an hour easing into the street, he hit the other car, and about a quarter of the other car fell to the concrete road. Several Mexicans jumped out of the car and pointed to their damaged car. Then they pointed toward Vance. This scene escalated, much shouting. No one in Vance's family could understand them. Jennifer rushed inside of the apartment house for help, someone who could understand the Mexicans who owned the damaged car. She found the top man. He simply waved his hand, and the irate Mexicans got in their car and left. He explained in English, "You were tricked, this is common in Mexico. The tricksters simply tie a part of a car together with wire or cord, and it falls off when another car only taps it. They are gone; they knew I would have them arrested."

Vance thought, *I was familiar with the trick a single Mexican used—he would "watch your car for a price."* Of course, what he meant was "if you don't pay me, I will do something to your car." Vance now had a new experience, which entailed pseudodamaging a car.

Vance and his family had many experiences in Mexico, but despite some of them, Vance learned many new things about electrocardiography.

54

Qualities Needed to Be Admitted

to Medical School

Vance Connelly met many young men and women who aspired to be admitted to medical school. With tongue in cheek, he made a list of characteristics that would clinch an acceptance to the best of schools. Vance collected some of the requirements from his colleagues, but most of these are his own:

- The candidate should have been a Boy Scout or Girl Scout and be known for helping the elderly cross a street.
- The candidate should have delivered newspapers early in the morning for at least six months, long enough to have to deal with irate customers.

- Each candidate should be asked to write an essay on how to tie his or her shoe. This would test the candidate's ability to communicate accurately.
- It would be a plus if the candidate's grandmother was obsessed with saving thread and buttons, because doctors can't keep up with anything. It is hoped that the grandmother's genes would enable the candidate to keep up with everything related to patient care.
- Should the candidate express the view that he or she detested sleeping, that confession would almost assure admittance to any medical school.
- Each candidate should be given a paragraph to read and be asked to state clearly, in his or her own words, what he or she read. When possible, the candidate should be asked how they would apply the information to solve a problem.
- The candidate should be asked to define what is a profession and to define *thinking, learning,* and *memory.*
- Candidates should be asked, "How do you learn?" Many students have memorized their way through college but may not have learned how to learn.

Some of these tongue-in-cheek suggestions are, of course, ridiculous, but even they carry an important message.

55

Daddy King

Dr. Vance Connelly saw Daddy King as a patient whenever King's primary care physician asked him to, but King occasionally called Vance at odd hours, day and night.

Vance really enjoyed Daddy King and studied him as a person as much as he studied and managed his illnesses. When he called, he never said who he was, but his clear and commanding voice was easy to recognize. His questions were to the point, and the conversation was always short. Sometimes he requested to see Vance, but most of the time, he only had a question.

One day, Daddy King called and said, "Come over here." Daddy King was at his home, suffering from the death of his wife. Vance moved quickly to his car and traveled the streets of Atlanta as fast as possible. A terrible event had occurred. Vance sensed the anguish that Daddy King was suffering. Daddy King's wife, who played the piano at their church, had been shot and killed by a mentally deranged man in the congregation.

Vance entered Daddy King's bedroom. He found Daddy King sitting up in bed. Vance expressed his sorrow and discovered that Daddy King had no physical complaints. There was no medical emergency, thank God.

Daddy King asked Vance to sit on the side of the bed. There was very little talking between them. After several minutes, Daddy King said, "Throw your legs up on the bed." Vance did so. So there they were both sitting in the bed. Again, very little talking. After a prolonged silence, Daddy King said, "I ain't gonna hate nobody." He said that several times. After a few minutes, perhaps ten or fifteen, Vance again expressed his sorrow and prepared to leave. Daddy King, in his great sorrow, simply looked at Vance as he left.

Vance never forgot Daddy King's words: "I ain't gonna hate nobody."

Vance learned a lot that day. He learned why Daddy King's son was nonviolent.

56

Poetry on the Radio

Vance and Jennifer had a maid, at least a part-time maid, that is, a *very* part-time maid. She sort of did what she wanted to do. She was rather large, but moved around gracefully, came when it was convenient, was not bashful, and spoke with a strong, commanding voice. She was unschooled but sent her daughter to an excellent university. She was street-smart, very street-smart. She did take courses, or so she said; she learned about the best products to use in her work. She would say, "I gotta stay up."

One day, she asked Vance, "I know you get up early, do you ever listen to me on the radio?"

Vance was taken aback. "What do you mean?" he asked.

"I read poetry on the radio at 5:00 AM."

"You do?"

With her hands on her rather round hips, she made it clear, "Yes, and I am good at it."

"My, my, what do they pay you?"

Her face dropped a little as she answered, "They don't pay me anything."

"Why do you do it?" Vance inquired.

"Power," she said with a clinched jaw, "power in my community."

Vance was not only surprised that she was on the radio, but also that she read poetry. The task performed just did not fit the one doing it. He listened at 5:00 AM. Yes, she was on the radio. Her voice was full and commanding. She could read beautifully, but what she read was far from emotionally charged poetry. She pulled it off, however, and her steady listeners liked what she did. Vance thought, *Good for her. She, in effect, was saying, "I will do fine in this screwed-up world we live in. I know what power is, don't mess with me."*

The last time Vance saw her was at Jennifer's memorial service. Vance asked her to sit with the family. She did—flowery dress, huge (very huge) hat, and all. At the reception, she shook hands with many friends and relatives. Last seen at the reception, she was filling a bag with cookies and other treats.

57

Turtles

Vance admitted that he knew little about turtles although he had a major in zoology and chemistry. He yielded to his six-year-old son Phil's desire to have a pet turtle.

Phil played with the turtle that was about three inches wide, dark green, with the usual interesting head and neck. As Vance remembers it, Phil was dutybound to feed the little turtle lettuce and water.

But tragedy lurked in the background. One day the turtle died. Phil was distraught. Jennifer, his mother, could not console him.

Phil finally said, "Call Jimmy Budd."

Jimmy Budd was our minister and friend. Jennifer knew he would understand. She called him. He came.

After placing his arms around Vance's youngest, Jimmy Budd decided he would help Phil bury the turtle. The two of them placed the turtle in a small matchbox, and with shovel in hand, they went into the woods located in the back of the Connelly home.

They buried the turtle. Although Vance was not at the service, one can be assured that an appropriate prayer was rendered. Knowing Jimmy Budd, we can all be sure it had an impact on Vance's six-year-old son.

The next day, Phil went to visit the turtle's grave. He ran back to the house. He told his mother that he saw an angel in one of the trees. She knew it was part of his childhood imagination.

Vance did not know how often Phil visited the grave, but he was pleased that Jimmy Budd had given his young son a lesson we might call the "reverence for life." Vance thought that Dr. Albert Schweitzer would be proud of both of them.

58

Who Made the Error?

Dr. Vance Connelly was not happy. He felt the results of an adrenaline surge. Morning report with the interns and residents jolted him because he encountered the following problem.

Intern Dr. Jed Jordon presented the problems of a patient who had been in the hospital a few days. He said, "I was not on duty last night, but this is what happened. Dr. Jones was covering for me and discovered that the patient, Mr. Josh Higgins, had a serum sodium of 120 mEq and gave him 1,000 cc of saline. The patient's heart failure got worse, he almost died."

Vance Connelly gritted his teeth, his look said it all, and he said, "There are very few things in medicine that you can state that you never do. Let me make this clear, you never give saline to a patient with heart failure. The low serum sodium is due to the retention of too much water, it dilutes the sodium."

Vance came close to yelling what he said, but he sensed that those in the room got the message.

Vance went to his office, sat at his desk, and pondered what he should do about such an error. As he cooled down, he heard a knock at the door. He opened the door and found the pale, sweating intern Dr. Jed Jordon standing there.

"Come in, Dr. Jordon, have a seat."

The intern sat a few feet from Vance and said nothing.

Dr. Connelly looked straight at him and said, "So."

"Dr. Connelly," he said, "I want to be sure you understand that I did not authorize the order for saline, I was checked out to Dr. Jones. I was distressed when I came in this morning and discovered what had happened. Fortunately, the patient is better now after giving him more diuretic. I am sorry this happened. I hate to say it, but every time I check out to Dr. Jones, something bad seems to happen. I just want to be sure that you understand that I did not do it."

Vance hung his head, closed his eyes, thought deeply about the problem, raised his head, looked deep into Dr. Jordon's eyes, and said, "You consider the patient to be yours?"

"Yes, sir."

"Does the patient think of you as his doctor?"

"Yes, sir."

Vance, knowing his next remark would never be forgotten, said, "Dr. Jordon, I hold you responsible for this error."

Dr. Jordon felt the chill of the moment, sweat popped out, pallor developed, and a quivering but soft voice said, "But, but, I was off duty."

Vance explained in several terse, well thought-out sentences, "Dr. Jordon, you said the patient was your patient. You also said that the patient viewed you as his doctor, and to the point, you said that each time you checked out to Dr. Jones, something bad happened. I submit, please hear me, that you should not check out to someone who has proven to you that they are over their head, so you are responsible for the error made on your patient."

The intern received the message, one that is not in the books—it is called responsibility. There is no such thing as partial responsibility, it is always total.

Vance then pondered how to improve the work of Dr. Jones. Was it the lack of knowledge, or was it the inability to apply knowledge, or was he in the wrong profession?

59

Red Roses

There was a red rose in a simple vase located on a table in the lobby of Atlanta's premier retirement home, Brookland. Occasionally there were two red roses there, and Dr. Vance Connelly had even seen three beautiful red roses in the vase.

The red rose was a signal that someone had died. Vance had learned that it could be someone he ate dinner with the night before. Vance understood that people over eighty years of age had already beaten the statistics; they were on borrowed time, whatever that means. Vance had also become accustomed to the recurrent fact that for several reasons, there were few people who planned to attend the services for the friend that had passed away. Most of the deceased's friends had already passed away, and those remaining had trouble navigating the bus ride that was provided, or they were incapacitated to the degree they could not walk.

But this time, the red rose was for Marcus. What a talented fellow. In his younger days, he was a radio announcer. Vance remembered his clear and distinctive voice. When Vance was about twelve years old, *Marcus and the Lone Ranger* dominated the radio waves.

Marcus could play the piano even though he was moderately deaf. He practiced in his room and would occasionally play for the residents at Brookland. He was ninety-eight years old when he died. He was still interesting. He wore interesting clothes and had a slightly younger girlfriend who had passed away a few months earlier.

Vance hung his head and closed his eyes as he stood before the red rose that symbolized a splendid life who touched many people for almost a century.

60

Unforgettable Utterances

Vance will never forget the sound of their voices, the grimaces of their faces, and the sweat on their brows.

Vance was eight to ten years of age. His father asked him to go with him to a small village to teach grown men how to read. Vance's father was a teacher during the Great Depression. He was principal of the school that he helped build. The Depression was in full force, and illiteracy was the rule. Vance learned to read before he entered school, and as a young kid, he had trouble understanding why some grown people could not read.

Vance and his father were out of school for the summer, so they jumped in their Model A Ford and went to a nearby village. They met about ten grown men in a church. The men wore the suits of the day, overalls. All of the men were African Americans. The men spoke and nodded when Vance's father entered the room.

Vance does not recall what prepared material his father handed them, but it was a list of simple words that were used every day. Vance remembers every detail of the effort the men exerted to pronounce the words. Vance's father would say the word; they looked at the word and tried to say it. Vance remembers one man, fifty to sixty years of age, struggling to say the word. Vance's father's hand was on his shoulder, and the man tried; he tried again, sweat appeared on his brow; he tried again, only utterance came. He continued, embarrassed and desperate but determined. When he finally said the word, Vance's father said, "Great," and patted him on his shoulder. The man smiled a large smile. Vance could see his rusty teeth. Vance's father smiled, as true teachers do when they succeed.

Epilogue

Our lives are filled with short, short stories. In fact, when the "sun sets" for good is when people identify with those who have left by telling stories about them. Here, in this little book, Dr. Vance Connelly (the pen name for the author), tells a few short, short stories that makes the point. I suggest that you, the reader, think about the stories that have made your life what it is. The stories may be funny or sad, but they are you. They separate you from all others.

CPSIA information can be obtained
at www.ICGtesting.com
Printed in the USA
LVHW091007220919
631862LV00001B/138/P

9 781441 581310